THE IN-BETWEEN

Angela Dunham

Copyright © 2017 ANGELA DUNHAM

All rights reserved.

ISBN-13: 978-0-692-05344-7

Dedication

This book is dedicated to my husband, Mark Dunham!

Love you, forever ever!

Acknowledgments

A big thank you to my mom, for being so obsessed with vampires, that I became obsessed with vampires. You started my love of the supernatural!

Thank you to my husband for your constant love and support. I don't know if I could have finished this book without it.

Thank you to my son Essex, for constantly reminding me of what's important in life. I hope you always look up to the stars and follow your dreams!

Thank you to all my friends who encouraged me to both start and finish this book. You know who you are!

Thank you to my friend and amazing editor, Ricardo Martinez. Without your help, I might not have had the confidence to self-publish!

Table of Contents

Prologue	Page	1
Chapter 1	Page	4
Chapter 2	Page	7
Chapter 3	Page	15
Chapter 4	Page	20
Chapter 5	Page	28
Chapter 6	Page	33
Chapter 7	Page	44
Chapter 8	Page	51
Chapter 9	Page	57
Chapter 10	Page	65
Chapter 11	Page	72
Chapter 12	Page	77
Chapter 13	Page	87
Chapter 14	Page	103
Chapter 15	Page	108
Chapter 16	Page	115
Chapter 17	Page	133
Chapter 18	Page	141
Chapter 19	Page	148

Chapter 20	Page	158
Chapter 21	Page	163
Chapter 22	Page	181
Chapter 23	Page	198
Chapter 24	Page	211
Chapter 25	Page	221
Chapter 26	Page	234
Chapter 27	Page	256
Chapter 28	Page	271
Chapter 29	Page	282
Chapter 30	Page	290
Chapter 31	Page	304
Chapter 32	Page	315
Chapter 33	Page	322
Chapter 34	Page	335
Epilogue	Page	345
About the Author	Page	349
Copyright	Page	350

Prologue

He woke up disoriented, blistering heat blasting all over his exposed skin. He tried to sit up but failed. His entire body ached. Feeling defeated, he just lay on the hard ground, panting. The air was humid and thick, making it uncomfortable to breathe. He had no recollection of where he was or what had happened to him. Peering out through blurry eyes that caked with sand, he saw a world on fire. What was going on? He wondered. The last thing he remembered was camping with his family. A million questions bombarded his mind. Had the bonfire gotten out of hand? Was there a forest fire? Oh god! He thought. Had his dad's propane tank exploded? Concerned for his family, he tried to sit up again, but the vertical motion caused him intense pain that he passed out instead.

Waking up the second time was far worse than the first. Along with the heat and pain, he now heard strange growling sounds coming from all around him. He knew bears frequented the area they were camping in, but these growls sounded off. It didn't matter what was making the noise; he was defenseless and needed to move. Adrenaline pumping, he managed to roll over onto his stomach and army crawl across the harsh sand. Scared and unable to see clearly, he aimed for the cover of what looked like woods. Once he made it under the thick canopy of trees, he took a few deep breaths before rolling onto his back again. It was painful, but he did it. Laying there, he tried to calm down and think. The last thing he remembered was unpacking the tent with his dad. Then, nothing. Did he have a concussion? He felt nauseous, wondering where everyone else was.

Something wet tickled his toes. Looking up, he saw a wall of blue fog rolling in towards him. Rubbing his hands over his eyes, he tried to see it more clearly. The mist appeared to be glowing, but that couldn't be, right?

He needed to find somewhere to clean up and wash all the gunk out of his eyes.

The fog moved in closer, slowly creeping up his body until it enveloped him completely. At first, the cold air felt nice against his warm skin. Then his lungs constricted violently. Rolling back over onto his stomach, he choked and coughed into the dirt. Grabbing onto his neck, he gasped as his throat began to close in on itself. Staring out into the woods, he prayed for help. Feeling his consciousness fade away, he fought to keep his eyes open. It was useless. He had no strength left. Before the world went completely dark, he saw the silhouette of enormous white wings coming towards him through the fog.

Chapter 1

It was the middle of December, freezing, and Ava Chase was miserable. Her family had recently relocated them to a new school, in a new town, with a new so-called life. All the changes may have been exciting for some, but all they caused were stress and anxiety for her. Change was her enemy, and this move was proving to be the biggest battle of her entire seventeen years.

A few months prior, her parents had decided to move them away from her childhood home in Florida to the frozen state of Colorado. Fox Field Colorado, to be exact. Just arriving at the airport had been a shock to the senses. In her opinion, whoever thought it was a good idea to put a giant purple horse with red laser beam eyes as a welcoming statue should be fired. It didn't help that the move was taking place in mid-December, the peak of winter. Florida was so hot and humid; it sometimes seemed ridiculous that human beings could even survive there. But now, so far away from home, she found herself missing the sweltering heat. Bye, Bye bikinis, hello ginormous fuzzy parkas. Well, parkas were a stretch, but still, there was a lot of claustrophobic layering going on.

Her eighteenth birthday was in three days. The age of freedom that every teen usually looked forward to. Except, this year, she didn't feel like celebrating. Turning the big one-eight without her best friend Kat was more than just depressing; it was tragic. Saying goodbye to her had been the worst part of the move, and Ava wasn't sure she could ever forgive her parents for splitting them up. They had phone and FaceTime dates, but it wasn't the same as seeing Kat's face in person. Nothing was the same.

Fox Field was just a tiny blip on the map, and she couldn't stand the small-town feel of the place. The town consisted of a handful of residential neighborhoods, three schools (an elementary school, middle school, and high school), one grocery store, one gas station, and three stoplights. Correction, make that, two stoplights. That was it! No gym, no salon, no restaurants, no SUSHI! Well, unless you counted "Mabel's Mountain Stop" as a restaurant, but that was pushing it. They served food, but nothing Ava considered "edible." The place was just a drinking hole for the truckers passing through town. Fox Field wasn't just an empty town; it was an isolated one. The commute from Fox Field to the hustle and bustle of downtown Denver was at least an hour, if you were speeding, and owned a car, which she currently did not. It was a testament to her power of self-preservation that she hadn't already died of boredom!

Chapter 2

It was Thursday, just another monotonous day at Lakeside High School. Shutting her locker door, she shoved her math book deep inside her backpack and bolted down the hallway. She was always late to class, and today was no exception. She was staring at the ground, weaving in and out of students, when she accidentally ran face-first into the wall. Embarrassed, she stood still for a moment, praying no one had noticed. Opening her eyes, she expected to find the wall, but instead, a black t-shirt with white writing met her line of vision. Confused, she looked up to find a person, not a wall. Mortified, she jumped backward, tripping over her own feet, before finally landing hard on the ground. Her butt took most of the impact, but the momentum sent her whole body flying backward, and her head hit the wall. Hard! Shocked, she just sat there for a few seconds in silence, breathing deeply. When she finally looked up to apologize to whoever it was, her brain shorted out.

The boy standing over her was beautiful, well, from what she could see of him. Everything was a wee bit fuzzy at the moment. She felt the back of her head, and there was already a good size knot forming. Beautiful sounded like a weird thing to call a guy, she thought. But hot or sexy didn't seem quite right. He was both of those things, in spades, but neither word fit him. He was tall, maybe 6'2, with broad shoulders and a lean muscular build. His hair was jet black, wavy, and a little unruly, curling up slightly at the ends. The messy look only managed to make him more appealing. His skin was smooth, olive-toned, and stood out in contrast with his dark hair. He had a flat, straight nose and perfectly shaped lips. When their eyes finally met, Ava let out a long breath and continued to sit on the ground, staring up at him like a complete dumbass. She just couldn't look away from his eyes. They were the most mesmerizing shade of green that she'd ever seen. An impossible mix between forest and emerald, framed by thick, dark lashes that most girls would die for. During the last two weeks at Lakeside, she'd never seen him before. His face was unforgettable.

After a lot more uncomfortable staring, she kind of expected him to help her stand up. Instead, he just stood there, arms crossed over his broad chest, glaring down at her. For a moment, she even swore his eyes were glowing, but that couldn't be right. Inwardly, she reminded herself that she might have a head injury and deemed it best to check in with the nurse before going to class.

"You should watch where you're going!" he growled.

His voice was deep, with a touch of an accent she was unfamiliar with. Confused, she managed to whisper, "yeah, maybe!"

Immediately upset with herself for not being more assertive, she added, "but what kind of guy knocks a girl over and doesn't even offer a hand?"

Her face felt hot, and she knew it was turning tomato red. It happened whenever she got upset.

She scrambled to pick herself up off the ground before anyone else noticed their exchange. When she finally stood up straight, she felt a slight pain in her left leg. Limping, she stepped closer to him, the top of her head barely reaching his shoulders. For some reason, she still expected him to say, "I'm sorry, or my bad," but nope, he just turned around and bolted in the opposite direction.

This time, anger gave her a voice. "I'll answer my question for you; it starts with a D and ends with the word bag!"

He didn't turn around. Maybe he thought his good looks made up for his lack of manners. Or maybe, he was just the D-bag she thought he was. Either way, she was insulted by his lack of concern and was now even later to class. Hoping the nurse would give her a pass, she limped down the hallway towards the administration offices, silently cursing her parents for putting her in this situation. The idea of having to finish out high school in this place, with people like him, made her want to cry. So far, her senior year was turning out to be just peachy. When she reached the administration hub, she found the nurse's office at the very end of the hall. The door was painted red and decorated with a white sign that read,

Headache, try W.O.W.

Water

Oxygen

Wait

She'd never had a headache before but filed the information under her "just in case" mental file. The door was open, and the nurse was standing over her desk, flipping through a binder.

Rapping lightly on the door, she called out, "Hello!"

The nurse turned around and smiled at her. She was a pretty, petite blonde, probably in her mid-forties.

"Good morning. I'm Nurse Elle; come on in and tell me what I can help you with."

Limping over to the small table, she sat down. "I slipped in the hallway a few minutes ago and thought I tweaked something in my left leg. I also hit my head, but it doesn't hurt. I just wanted to get checked out before I head to class."

Nurse Elle pulled out a small light pen from the pocket of her coat. "I'm so sorry to hear that. Let's give you a good look-see."

The nurse flashed the light in her left eye and then the right while asking, "Look up, down, left, and right for me."

Then she felt around her head, behind both ears, and down both sides of her neck. "You have a big knot on the back of your head. Do you have a headache, blurred vision, nausea, or feel confused?"

Currently, she didn't have any of those symptoms, but that rude boy had seemed a little fuzzy right after she'd hit her head. Then again, she also thought his eyes were glowing. Deciding it was probably better to keep that information to herself, she lied. "No!"

"Good!" Nurse Elle replied, "Now, let's have a look at that leg."

Nurse Elle carefully lifted her leg into the air, turning it to the left and then to the right, "Is there any pain when I do this?"

Wincing, she said, "A little when you turn it to the right."

Nurse Elle nodded, "I think you bruised your left hip, and it's causing a little discomfort in your leg. I don't think it's anything serious, but have your parents take you to the doctor if the pain is worse tomorrow. I'm going to grab an ice pack. I want you to sit here for fifteen minutes, icing that side, and then let me know if you feel good enough to go back to class. If not, I'll go ahead and contact your parents."

Ava cringed at the thought of calling her parents. Her mom was working in Denver, and her dad was busy with a ton of jobs that day. Not wanting to burden either of them, she lied to the nurse fifteen minutes later and said she was okay. As she headed back to class with her late excuse in hand, her leg and hip still hurt a little, but the limp was gone. Thankfully, she'd always been a fast healer.

Chapter 3

Second-period calculus with Mr. White was her least favorite class. Mr. White had to be the most boring teacher in the history of the world. His incessant talking would drone on and on until the only math problem you could remember was one plus one equals; I want to stab myself in the face. The only positive thing about his class was that Olivia was in it. Since starting school two weeks ago, she had found it difficult to connect with anyone. Partly because of guys like the one this morning and partly because she was super shy. On her first day, when Mr. White had introduced her to the class, Olivia, or Liv as everyone called her, had immediately volunteered to help her learn the ropes. Liv had given her a school tour, helped her find all her classes, and even sat with her at lunch. Liv was sweet, easy-going, friendly, and wait for it, drama-free! That was rare! Liv was a keeper!

As usual, Mr. White was in the middle of a lecture and glared at her as she passed by his desk. She was late all the time, and he was clearly over it. After dropping the yellow excuse slip on his desk, she took her seat.

"Morning!" she whispered to Liv as she plopped down in her desk chair.

Liv sat behind her and was in the middle of thumbing through her calculus book, looking as confused as Ava felt most days in this class.

Liv was a beautiful girl, with big brown eyes and the cutest little button nose. But poor Liv had astigmatism and was forced to wear coke bottle thick glasses 24/7, that hid most of her pretty face. She had long brown hair that was perfectly straight and perfectly silky smooth. Like, All. The. Time! Hers was a wavy hot mess on a good day.

"Hey girl," Liv whispered back, "Is everything okay? I mean, you're always late, but class is almost over. And by the way, is it lunchtime yet? I'm starving?"

As Liv said the words aloud, her stomach growled in agreement.

Ava wasn't sure why Liv never ate breakfast. By second period, she was always starving. After two weeks of the same routine, she came prepared for this very situation. Pulling a granola bar out of her bag, she tossed it onto Liv's desk. "We wouldn't want famine to take you before lunch."

Liv giggled. A little too loudly, causing Mr. White to turn around from scribbling on the chalkboard to shoot her a look of death. On that note, Ava turned around in her seat and pulled out her textbook.

"You're late again, Miss Chase!" Mr. White said, using his authoritative tone. Or big boy voice as she liked to joke.

Instead of responding with a smartass comment, she chose the high road, flashing him puppy dog eyes.

"Sorry, Mr. White. I had an excuse today, and it's right there on your desk."

Rolling his eyes, he said, "Next time your late, excuse or not, you'll be spending the remainder of the day in detention."

Mr. White continued to glare at her for another moment as if the extra second would make his point hit home. Finally satisfied, he turned around and continued with his boring lesson about quadric equations. She tried to focus but quickly got distracted by the loud crunching sounds coming from behind her. Smiling to herself, she scribbled down the equation, thankful for her four-eyed friend Liv.

Chapter 4

When the bell finally rang, Ava and Liv beelined it to the lunchroom. When Liv was hangry, she was the worst at being patient, and the longer it took them to get to the lunchroom, the longer the lines would be. Without quick access to food, sweet little Liv would turn into a tiny wolverine on steroids. She liked to call it hypoglycemic rage syndrome, or H.R.S. Not to be confused with child protective services. Although, children might need protection if they get between Liv and her food.

Dodging students left and right, they rushed toward the blue double doors at the end of the hall. The lunchroom was exactly like any other dull cafeteria, with beige walls and row after row of white plastic tables. Ava eyed the line. BINGO! It was super short. Liv always went for sweets; first, today being no exception. As she piled her tray high with two puddings and a doughnut, Ava gaped in horror. If she ate like that, her ass would expand on the spot. How tiny Liv managed to stay bean pole skinny while constantly inhaling all kinds of refined sugar and fat defied logic. She inwardly cursed at how unfair life could be. Cafeteria lunches across the Country had become better balanced since Michelle Obama's "Let's Move" initiative started. However, Lakeside still had a lot of unhealthy options on the menu. Today, she opted for a whole-wheat turkey sandwich and a bowl of sliced cucumbers.

Their lunch table was in the very back of the room, near a long wall of floor-to-ceiling windows that looked out over the lawn. Currently, there was no lawn to speak of, only patches of brown dirt mixed with patches of white melting snow. As they approached the table, Liv waived to Adam and Gabe. Adam was of average height, with bleach-blond hair and wide blue eyes. He had that All-American thing going on and was captain of The Purple Foxes, Lakeside's soccer team. Every sports team at the

Lakeside wore bright purple on purple uniforms, and it was purple overkill.

Adam was always friendly to her and Liv but tended to get confrontational over little things with his other friends. He was also super passionate about soccer. Once you got him talking about it, it was go time! He could go on for hours about who was playing who, what teams you should like, blah, blah, blah!

Gabe was seated next to him as usual. They were best friends and total opposites. Gabe was tall, lean, and had probably never played a sport in his entire life. He had wavy brown hair that was always a hot mess because he constantly ran his fingers through it. He also had an ever-abundant stock of t-shirts that were always wrinkled. Pretty much everything about him screamed "I don't give a shit!" Rewind to the t-shirt topic. Every single one he owed was an ode to a comic book, superhero, or sci-fi fantasy something or other. He was a total geek and owned it! Liv said his bedroom was lined floor to ceiling with action figures, but Ava had yet to see the shrine for herself. He seemed like a nice down to earth guy who would do just about anything for his friends.

In her opinion, the other kids at the table weren't so great. There was Megan, Adam's current girlfriend, and the stereotypical mean girl. She was completely self-absorbed and seemed to have a never-ending case of P.M.S. Ava didn't understand how Liv was such good friends with her but to each their own. In her imagination, she pictured Megan bribing Liv with Little Debbie snacks or some other kind of snack food in exchange for friendship. Yeah, that had to be it, she thought.

Finally, there was Haven. Rumor had it she was a witch, a psychic, or possibly just a weirdo, and she always wore black. Black clothes, black lipstick, heavy black eyeliner, black jewelry; you name it, she had it in black. It was easy for people to make up fanciful stories to keep themselves occupied in a small town with nothing much to do. To date, she had never even talked to Haven. The few times she'd attempted to say hello, the girl just gave her an awkward wave and quickly looked away. It was strange. Haven and Megan never talked either, and it seemed like Megan only tolerated Haven's presence because of Liv. Liv, the ever sweet, seemed to be the glue that held this mishmash group of people together.

When they sat down, Adam and Gabe were already in the middle of a heated discussion about Devil's Head Lake. It was the closest lake to the town and a source of mystery here in Fox Field. Apparently, over the last decade, numerous people had gone missing after going into the water. But so far, no bodies had ever been recovered. The last incident had been a few years back when one of Gabe and Adam's friends had gone missing. The police had labeled it a drowning, but his body was never found, just like all the others.

"It didn't happen that way! Your sister made it up!" Adam yelled across the table. For best buds, Adam and Gabe sure did fight a lot. In the past two weeks, she had witnessed at least five of these spats.

Gabe pushed his lunch tray aside, spilling apple sauce all over the floor. "We've been over this so many times, and I'm tired of talking about it. Holly was with him when it happened, and I believe her. You saw how freaked out she was!"

Holly was Gabe's younger sister and a freshman.

Adam rolled his eyes. "Holly was too young to know what she saw. I remember waking up when she ran into our campsite, screaming. It's time for you to accept it for what it is. Kade drowned! Just like those other people. It was horrible, and we lost our friend, but it isn't the big cover-up you're trying to make it out to be. There is a logical explanation for why no bodies have been recovered. FFPD only hired a few certified divers to search the lake, and they missed something. I'm telling you, the bodies are stuck down there somewhere; they just can't find them!"

Adam stood up, continuing with his rant, "You're trying to turn the whole thing into some big story, but this isn't one of your comics, and Kade isn't Aqua Man. He just drowned! Damn it, Gabe! Just let it go!"

Done with the conversation, Adam turned around and stomped off.

Gabe rearranged his tray, picked up his fork, and started stabbing at a rogue pea. "He can be such a dick sometimes!"

Ava flashed him a reassuring smile, but he was staring down at his plate, clearly lost in thought. The fight left everyone feeling a little uncomfortable, and they all ate in silence for the rest of the lunch hour.

The remainder of the school day went by without any additional drama. As the hours passed, Ava went from class to class, feeling detached from reality. For some reason, she kept daydreaming about the A-hole from that morning. Making a mental note to ask Liv about him later, Ava tried unsuccessfully to focus on her English paper. She just couldn't get his image out of her head. Especially his eyes. The impressive green ones she'd sworn were glowing. When the last bell rang, it startled her so badly that she jumped out of her chair. As the other kids giggled and snickered, all she could think was, could this day get any worse!?

Chapter 5

Ava waited for Liv outside the school, at their usual meeting spot. Lakeside High was a one-story, red brick building nestled on the East side of town. She lived three blocks away from the school in the same subdivision as Liv. After her first day, they had agreed to start walking together. Many of the other students had cars or parents who picked them up, but she and Liv weren't so lucky. Liv's parents were older, retired, and always vacationing here or there, leaving Liv in the care of her older brother, Alex. At twenty, he had just started taking college classes online and was a tad self-involved, never thinking to offer Liv a ride when it was freezing out. On the flipside, Liv never wanted to bother him.

Her parents were workaholics and could never get home in time for dinner, let alone to pick her up from school. So, here they were, two frozen peas in a pod, walking home on the brink of frostbite. Her teeth were chattering so badly that it made it hard to speak.

Sputtering, she said, "So, I saw this guy at school today that I've never seen before. He would be hard to miss. Burr, damn, it's cold! What I mean is, he was, really, good-looking. He has dark hair with these crazy green eyes. I mean, his eyes were so green it was freaky. Good looks aside, he was rude and practically tackled me in the hallway. Do you know anyone who fits that description?"

Liv glared at her; one brow lifted. "Seriously, you wait until now to tell me some hot guy tackled you in the hallway. Information like that is an E-News alert around here, and not a wait until the end of the day kind of thing!"

Ava laughed, but it sounded more like a weird cackle through her chattering teeth. "Well, I couldn't tell you in Mr. White's class after getting in more trouble.

Then Gabe and Adam were fighting at lunch, so it slipped my mind. I'm telling you now!"

Liv was quiet for a minute, then said, "I don't think I know him. I mean, if he's as hot as you say, then everyone would know him, right? Our school is way too small for a hottie in hiding. If he's a new student, wouldn't he have been at lunch with us today? My best guess? He's not a student at all. He's probably some faculty member's kid or has a sibling he was dropping off."

Liv's voice sounded muffled, and when she looked over at her, she couldn't see Liv's face at all. Her scarf completely covered it up, and only her glasses were still showing.

"Yeah, maybe." Ava laughed, pulling her own scarf over her mouth and nose.

She secretly hoped Liv was right. If the mystery guy had a parent or a sibling at their school, she might run into him again. Literally. Liv's house was up first. It was a large, Victorian-style mini-mansion that sat on a huge corner lot looking grand. Liv's house stood out because it was the only purple one in the subdivision. These Coloradans sure did love them some purple—all the homes in their community were new but built to mimic the old Victorian era. The houses were pretty to look at, but knowing they weren't historic took away from the charm.

Liv began walking up to her driveway, blowing into her already gloved hands out of habit. "Do you want to come in for a while? I can make us some hot cocoa."

Hot Cocoa sounded good, but she had a ton of homework to do, and her parents would lose it if she fell behind. "No thanks, I should get home. Raincheck?"

"Okey-doke," Liv said as she sprinted the last few steps to her front door. Just before she went inside, she turned back and yelled, "Before I forget, are you free

Saturday? It's supposed to warm up a little, and Gabe wants to go to Devil's Head Lake for a picnic. I think that place is creepy, but he seems excited. Please come with me?"

It hadn't escaped her attention that Gabe was always starring at Liv. In a way that screamed, I want to be more than just friends. So, she wasn't sure if going with them was the best idea.

"Liv, are you sure he doesn't think it's a date?"

Liv's eyes shot open wide like she'd never even considered it. "Well, I hope not. Even if I did want to go on a date with him, which I don't. I wouldn't be swooning over a date at Devil's Head Lake. So just do a girl a solid and just come with, pretty please!?!"

Spending the day as a third wheel sounded like torture, but she still found herself saying, "I'll think about it," as she waved goodbye.

Chapter 6

After saying goodbye to Liv, Ava beelined it down the sidewalk. The wind was picking up, and her house was still a few streets away. With every freezing gust, she felt like she was inhaling ice crystals. Since moving to Fox Field, most days had been like this one. Dreary and frozen, with no sun in sight. Even the few times the sun had made an appearance, the scenery still wasn't anything special. All the trees were barren this time of year, and the ground was constantly covered in snow or mud. She'd never seen snow before the move, and man, was it overrated! Pretty, yes! But it was always accompanied by bone-chilling cold and soggy wet conditions. Trying to find some light in her dark situation, she focused on the vast mountain range that dotted the entire south side of Fox Field.

The mountains were one of the few things she did appreciate. For some reason, staring at them always made her feel calm. Pausing for a moment, she watched in awe as a vast, misty gray storm cloud rolled over the side of one. Glancing around, she tried to imagine what the town might look like during Springtime when all the trees were lush and full of life. Florida didn't have seasons unless you counted hot and hotter. But living here, she would finally get to experience them all. A Summer where you didn't sweat to death. A Fall where you got to see the leaves change color. It all sounded great, but she still missed home. Florida had been the home she'd known for the past seventeen years.

    Her mom was a museum curator and had taken a position with an art gallery in Denver. Hence the move. Her dad was an electrician and could pretty much work anywhere, so when her mom got the job offer, they jumped at the opportunity. Her dad still hadn't found a permanent job in Fox Field but kept busy doing odd jobs for anyone who would hire him. Instead of moving straight to Denver, where the museum was, her mom had picked

Fox Field. She said she liked the idea of Ava going to a smaller school, where she could focus more on her studies and less on her social life. In her opinion, that line of thinking was total B.S.! Even at her old school, she'd always kept up decent grades, but her mom was a perfectionist who wanted her to follow suit. Anything less than straight A's was unacceptable.

Her mom's long commute to work, mixed with her crazy hours at the museum, made it nearly impossible for them to spend any quality time together. Not that they had in Florida either. Her parents always made work their number one priority in any zip code. Her dad was usually home in the evenings, but being home didn't always mean being present. When she'd been a little girl, he'd always been there, her knight in shining armor, ready to battle the monsters in her closet and kiss all her boo-boos away. But as the years passed by, he seemed less and less interested in keeping a close relationship with her. He always went through the motions of asking, "how was your day? "or "how did you do on the test?" But, beyond that, they barely spoke these days. Sometimes, she wondered if it was because she was a teenager, and other times she wondered if it was because she was adopted. Her parents had adopted her when she was a baby, and growing up, it hadn't mattered. Being a young child, they were all she knew, biological or not. But now, she felt like an outsider in their home.

When she finally reached her house, she raced across the snow-covered grass, leaving a trail of footprints in her wake. Unlocking the front door, she stepped inside the front foyer, unable to move for a few minutes while her body convulsed uncontrollably. After the shaking stopped, she took off her winter coat, hanging it up inside the front closet. Then, she quickly pulled off her boots and left them to dry near the front door. The inside of their home reflected her mom's tastes, all contemporary and artsy with grey walls and minimalist furniture. It felt cold, just like their relationship. Shrugging off the bad feelings, she headed into the kitchen to grab a drink. There was a yellow sticky note stuck to the fridge, scribbled in her dad's handwriting: Leftovers in the fridge. The snowstorm knocked out some transformers last night. Be home late.

Typical, she thought, as she popped the top on her grape soda. Placing the leftover lasagna in the microwave to reheat, she sat down at the kitchen island to read over her math notes. Her note-taking skills were proving to be useless since she couldn't read half of her handwriting. Frustrated with herself, she added, "writing more neatly" to her mental list of things to work on.

After scarfing down the food and cleaning up, she beelined it to her room, excited for her daily phone call with Kat. They alternated between regular phone calls and Facetime. Today, she was in more of a phone call/Bluetooth kind of mood so that she could multitask.

She hadn't had a lot of friends back in Florida, but it never really bothered her. Having a Kat was like having an army at your side. In her opinion, having one friend that always had your back was far better than five who didn't.

They'd met on the first day of kindergarten and instantly hated each other. Hair pulling and name-calling had ensued, which, if Ava remembered correctly, was all Kat's fault! Then again, if you asked Kat, she had an entirely different version of the story that included Ava spitting on her. You say tomato, and I say to-mah-to. As a result, their teacher, Mrs. Marsh, forced them to sit at the same table and interact daily. It turned out they had a lot in common, and by the end of the school year, they were attached at the hip. She thanked Mrs. Marsh for that gift every day!

Sitting on the end of her bed, she pulled out her cell phone and called her lifeline.

Kat answered on the second ring. "Helloooo! It's Kat the Christmas elf. What's your favorite color?"

Smiling, Ava said, "Hello Mrs. Fancy pants, how was your day?"

Kat sang her response loudly! "Not too eventful, and I decided to sing everything today. Signing makes everything better, don't you think?"

Her intro song was then proceeded by many other songs describing her entire day in agonizing detail, starting with an ode to oatmeal and ending with a horrible attempt at opera. The last one left Ava wishing she had some earplugs. No matter how bad things seemed, Kat could always make them better. They talked for a while about this and that, including her hot guy encounter and Kat's ever-annoying boyfriend. Why Kat kept dating the idiot was beyond her realm of understanding. All he ever did was drive her insane. Even though she cherished her talks with Kat, it was always a catch twenty-two. Hearing Kat's sweet voice always made Ava miss her that much more. After saying goodbye, she headed into the bathroom for a quick shower.

As the hot water eased the leftover chill in her bones, she couldn't help but feel a pinch of jealousy towards her friend. Kat was still in Florida, with a boyfriend to boot! Annoying as he might be, she had never had a boyfriend or even been on an actual date. Her only claim to fame had been in ninth grade when she went to see a movie with Toby Fisher. What a disaster that had been! After he repeatedly tried to grope her lady parts, poor Toby ended up with a big black eye. Of course, his version of the story was quite different. The next day at school, he told everyone that she had gone bat shit crazy when he brought her a Sprite instead of a Coke, resulting in her throwing the cup in his face. After that, no one had ever asked her out again. She'd been interested in a few guys since then but could never muster up the courage to approach them first.

After the shower, she wrapped herself up in her soft white bathrobe and headed back into her bedroom. Her room was the only place in the house that felt cozy and inviting. The walls were painted in a deep shade of maroon that offset her crisp, white bedsheets, and colorful pictures and prints that she'd collected over the years decorated the top of her dresser. There was a huge bay window in the corner that overlooked the backyard. Bright white curtains framed the windows around it, and the plush bench seat underneath it was her favorite spot to cozy up with a book. Her queen-sized bed housed way too many throw pillows for one person ever to need, but she didn't care. She loved snuggling up in her sheets and getting lost in the sea of pillows.

Walking over to her dresser to grab a change of clothes, she caught her reflection in the mirror. Since the move, she hadn't been sleeping well, and it showed. Without any makeup on, the dark circles under her eyes popped out against her olive-toned skin. She'd never thought of herself as pretty, but she wasn't unattractive either. On a scale of one to ten, she rated herself a five. Her dark brown hair was wavy and fell just above her shoulders. One of the few pluses to moving to Fox Field was that she had better hair. Back in Florida, with all the humidity, it had taken a gallon of product and an hour of flat ironing to tame her unruly locks. Now, it looked smooth and shiny without much effort.

She was petite, barely 4" 11,' with a small oval face, straight nose, and a bottom lip that was slightly fuller than the top. The only thing out of the ordinary was her eye color. Her eyes were jet black, with no pupils in sight. She had pupils, of course, but her eyes were so dark that they right blended in. Since moving, she hadn't been asked out or hit on at all. Too bad she couldn't still blame it all on Toby Fisher.

She'd always been a little self-conscious about her eyes. Not because she didn't like them, but because she'd never met anyone else with eyes as dark as hers. Maybe they made her seem unapproachable, or perhaps she was just reaching and needed to chill. It wasn't like she was jonesing for a boyfriend or anything. Done obsessing about it for the moment, she slipped on her pajamas and sat down at her desk to get started on her homework.

Chapter 7

As Ava walked by Liv's house the following day, Liv wasn't waiting for her on the corner. That seemed unusual since they walked together every day. The temperature had dropped drastically overnight, so she assumed Liv was just avoiding the cold and waiting inside. Her cell phone was buried deep in her backpack, and rather than dig it out, she walked up to Liv's front door and knocked several times, but no one answered. After waiting for a few more minutes, she peeked inside the long glass panel on the right side of the door. From there, she could see into the living room, which was empty.

Frustrated and cold, she walked around the side of the house to check the driveway. Alex's car wasn't there. That wasn't surprising since he stayed the night at his girlfriend's house often, but still, his absence made her feel uneasy. Before giving up completely, she dug out her cell phone and called Liv, but it went straight to voice mail.

Hanging up, she tried the landline, but there was no answer there either. It just rang and rang until the machine finally picked up. She left messages on both phones for Liv to call her back ASAP, and with no other options short of breaking in, she headed off to school. It concerned her that Alex left Liv home alone most nights, but every time she offered to let Liv sleepover, she nicely declined. As she walked down the driveway, she kept her fingers crossed that Liv was just sick and resting. It was flu season, after all, and half the kids at Lakeside already had it

    She was still a few streets away from school when the sky began to darken, and the temperature took a massive nosedive. Confused, she picked up the pace. The morning news hadn't mentioned an approaching storm, and the sky looked clear just a second before. Out of nowhere, the wind blew so hard it knocked her over. Falling hard on her butt, she slid on the slick ice, sliding around, until finally landing face-first in a large bank of snow. Spitting and cursing, she stood up, surrounded by total darkness. Completely blind, she reached out wildly, trying to feel around for anything, but only grasped thin air. Along with the blindness came total silence. There were no sounds of the cars passing by, no banging from the construction site in the distance, and no drip-drop of the ice melting onto the frozen sidewalk. She took a few clumsy steps forward, still hoping to find something to anchor her. Panicked, she didn't understand what was happening and wondered if she somehow damaged her eyes and ears in the fall. Neither hurt, but there was no other explanation for her current situation.

The air around her began to freeze and solidify until it felt like she was walking through a giant slushy. She was freezing, her entire body shaking from the arctic sheen of ice pressing against it. When she tried to take another step, it was impossible to move through the thick icy air. Terrified, she pushed all her weight forward and tried to lift her arms. At first, nothing happened. Refusing to give up, she kept trying to raise her arms until a strange warming sensation pooled in both of her hands. The feeling was brief, but after it passed, her arms slid effortlessly through the ice. Then very, very slowly, she began to inch her way forward. After a few pained steps, she was finally free from whatever had trapped her. Still blind and deaf, she ran! Heart racing, it took all her focus just to plant one foot in front of the other. Even her heavy footfalls didn't make a sound as she pushed her burning legs faster, trying to get away from wherever she was.

Lungs burning, she stopped running in an attempt to catch her breath. When she did, her sight and hearing came back just as quickly as they had left her. Looking around, she was shocked to find herself standing in the middle of a very long, unfamiliar street. The gray brick walls on both sides of the road soared up farther than her eyes could see. Confused, she turned around to try and gauge where she'd come from, but the street looked the same in both directions. Unsure of what to do, she kept walking in her current direction. The road seemed to go on forever until she finally reached a slight bend. When she rounded the corner, it was more of the same tall brick walls, but now, she could hear what sounded like rushing water in the distance.

Relieved that her senses were back in action, she followed the sound, hoping it was the city water plant. As she moved closer to the noise, the air began to smell bad. As she walked, the smell became so intense that she had to cover her nose and mouth with both hands to avoid vomiting. She hadn't noticed before, but now, she wondered if the water plant and dump were right next to each other. To her, that seemed like a bad idea, with potential for a lot of contamination issues, but what did she know?

Suddenly, a small glowing white light appeared up ahead, at what she hoped was the end of the road. When she reached the end of the pavement, the road transformed into a narrow, slick, rocky ledge. Transfixed by the light, she slowly walked out onto the ledge, only to find herself standing in the middle of a vast cavern. The sound of rushing water was coming from a choppy river below her, and the light was floating in the middle of the room. All around her, bright orange and red flames licked up the sides of the cavern, disappearing into the ceiling above.

As the floating light moved in closer, it began to pulse brightly until finally blinking out completely. Left in its place was a tall shadowy figure. It was a man, Ava could tell that from the build, but she couldn't make out anything else because he was facing the opposite direction. In that moment, she snapped out of whatever daze had prompted her to walk onto the ledge in the first place. Realization dawned that she was lost and alone with some strange man. Just as she stepped backward, attempting to put some distance between them, the man turned around and walked towards her.

Their eyes met, and his were the same brilliant shade of green that she'd seen the day before at school. Her breath left her lungs, and she felt stunned under his gaze. His expression seemed hurt and desperate as he stared back at her.

"Avaaaaa...." he whispered.

Even though his mouth hadn't moved, she somehow knew it was his voice. Her name echoed through the cavern, repeating over and over. Louder, softer, on the left, then the right. Terrified, she turned around and ran back down the road as fast as her legs would carry her. The brick walls lining the street closed in on her quickly, and right before the walls crushed her completely, she released a blood-curdling scream!

Chapter 8

Ava was still screaming when she woke up in her bed, covered in sweat. Startled, she pushed the wet hair out of her face and took a few deep breaths, attempting to calm down. She wasn't prone to nightmares, and most of her recurring dreams were too uneventful to remember. This one, though, this one, felt so real! Her nose was still burning, and she swore she could still smell that godawful stink from the dream. The smell was familiar somehow, but she couldn't quite place it at first. After a few big whiffs of her arm, it finally came to her. Eggs, her arm smelled just like rotten eggs. Gross, she thought!

She had no idea why her skin would smell like rotten eggs. It wasn't just her skin. No, the entire room reeked. The only logical explanation was that the eggs in the fridge had gone bad. She'd never had a smell manifest itself into a dream before, but there was a first time for everything. Begrudgingly, she got out of bed to check things out.

After a thorough investigation of the kitchen and no eggs in sight, she was even more confused. Searching the rest of the house, she concluded that the foul odor was only in her room. She wanted to check the backyard to see if the smell was wafting in from outside her bedroom window, but the idea of trudging through the snow this early in the morning was a no-go. Instead, she headed back to her room, turned on the ceiling fan, and sprayed everything down with Febreze. If the smell was wafting in from outside, she didn't want to open the window and make things worse. Plus, it was super frigid out.

Glancing over at the clock on her bedside table, she was shocked to see it was already 7:15 AM. She'd somehow slept right through her alarm. To be on time for school, she'd have to be walking out the door that very moment. Feeling stressed, she contemplated staying home.

Just thinking about breaking the rules made her stomach flutter with worry. She'd never taken a sick day, let alone skipped, and if her parents found out, they'd probably kill her. Weighing the pros and cons, she decided a day of relaxation trumped her chances of getting caught. Decision made, she called Liv to give her a heads up. They were supposed to be meeting on the corner in T-minus two minutes, and she didn't want her to worry. Liv answered on the second ring,

"Morning! You must have ESP! I was just about to call you when I noticed you weren't walking down the street. Is everything alright?"

"Yes," she answered, "I mean, I think so. I just had a bad dream last night and slept through my alarm. I don't want to get into all the specifics right now, but since it's Friday, I'm just going to stay home and catch up on some sleep."

Yawning, she laid back down on her bed.

Liv sighed, "You're really going to leave me alone with Mr. White? If I didn't love you so much, I'd walk down there and bitch smack you!"

Smiling, she pulled her throw blanket up over her legs. "Cranky today, are we?"

Liv snorted, "A little. You can make it up to me by going to the lake with us tomorrow."

She tried to think of a good reason to say no, but nothing came to mind. Feeling cornered, she caved. "Fine! I'll go! But if Gabe gets upset, you're dealing with him!"

"Agreed! Just be at my house by eleven and make sure to dress warmer than usual. It's always colder up there." Liv huffed.

Rolling her eyes, she said, "Great! This situation just keeps getting better and better. See you then!"

The last thing she wanted to do was get frostbite while hanging out by a creepy lake, but sometimes you had to make sacrifices for your friends. This was one of those times. After ending the call, she tried to fall back asleep, but every time she closed her eyes, she felt the panic of those walls closing in on her. After tossing and turning in bed for almost an hour, she finally gave up, kicking the blankets to the floor in frustration.

Now that she had an entire day to fill, she didn't know what to do with herself. All of her homework was done, and sleeping wasn't going to happen. With nothing else to do, she decided to brave the negative morning temperature and check outside for the source of the smell. After pulling on her rain boots and bulky winter coat, she headed out through the sliding glass doors in the kitchen.

Their back yard was a decent size and surrounded by a six-foot-high privacy fence. In the summer, she could imagine her mom putting out the nice patio furniture and unwinding back here with a glass of wine. Currently, the yard was empty, except for the blanket of crisp, white snow covering the ground. Thick, wet snow that she now had to trudge through. Once she reached her window, she sniffed all around the sill, and there was still nothing. She wasn't sure of too many things that smelled like rotten eggs, except for well water, and their community was on city. Convinced the smell must be coming from another house, she headed back inside. If the smell persisted, she would mention it to her parents. For now, there was nothing else she could do.

Feeling a little defeated, she grabbed the smelly sheets off her bed and shuffled to the laundry room. While they were washing, she straightened up her room and cracked open a novel she'd been reading for the past few weeks. It was a paranormal romance, her favorite!

Chapter 9

In the middle of an exciting chapter, Ava heard the front door open and shut. Startled, she peeked out of her bedroom door and caught a glimpse of her dad walking across the front foyer. A huge lump rose in her throat, and she felt like vomiting. Her parents were adamant about doing well in school and would freak out if they caught her skipping. The way she saw it, she only had two options. She could hide out in her room until 4:00 PM, then crawl out the window, walk around to the front of the house, and come back in through the front door. Or, sneak out now to find somewhere else to kill time.

Before she could decide, her dad yelled down the hall, "Ava, I know you're in there!

Dammit, she thought, caught red-handed. She had no idea how he knew she was home.

In a shaky voice, she responded, "Yeah, Dad, I'm....um, in here."

He pushed her bedroom door open, sticking just his head inside. He was wearing his favorite Met's hat, and his unruly blonde curls were sticking out underneath. His hair's current length was about all her mom would tolerate before forcing him to cut it. Personally, she liked the messy look.

"Why are you home, sweetie? Is everything alright?" he asked, clearly concerned.

She decided honesty was the best policy, "Dad, please don't be mad! I had a horrible dream last night and slept right through my alarm. I know that's a lame excuse, but the dream really freaked me out. How did you know I was here anyway?"

He stepped fully inside the room. "Your backpack is hanging up by the front door, and the washing machine is running. Since your mom is at work, I didn't think a burglar would be doing laundry. You're right though, having a bad dream isn't a good excuse to miss school. Consider yourself grounded for the weekend!"

She expected him to be mad but was surprised by the grounding. "Seriously, Dad? I've never skipped or missed a day of school in my entire life! Can't you just cut me some slack this once? I promised Liv I'd go to the lake with her tomorrow and don't want to let her down!"

He crossed his arms over his chest, glaring over at her. "Well, you should have thought about that before you skipped. You can also lose the attitude, or I'll add a whole week to your punishment. Your mom and I don't ask very much of you, and you should have called one of us to let us know what happened. You can use the weekend to catch up on schoolwork you missed today!"

Frustrated, she slammed her book closed. "This is so unfair! I have straight A's!! Missing one day of school isn't going to change that!"

Ignoring her protest, he left the room without another word, slamming the door shut behind him.

Later that evening, she lay in bed, trying to stay awake until her mom came home. Her mission sweet talk her into letting her go the lake since her dad was being completely unreasonable. She knew it was a long shot, but Sunday was her birthday, and maybe, just maybe, her mom would cave if she played her cards right. By 10:45 PM, her mom still hadn't come home, and her eyelids were getting heavy. Refusing to give up, she turned on the radio, hoping the noise would keep her awake, but after fifteen minutes, sleep finally won.

The lake's surface was so black that it looked like polished glass, mirroring the sky, the mountains, and her reflection. Her feet dangled over the side of an old rickety dock, and this time, she somehow knew she was dreaming. The lake was huge, serene, and surrounded by beautiful white snow-capped mountains. They reminded her of the range she saw every day from Fox Field. In the distance, where two of the mountains met, a deep valley gave the illusion that the lake stretched on forever in between it. It was eerily quiet, and she felt a sense of peace just watching the reflection of the clouds on the water's surface.

After hearing all the stories about Devil's Head Lake, she had done tons of research and discovered the origin of the lake's name. When early settlers first stumbled upon this area, they thought the two adjoining mountains looked like the face of a demon. They described the two mountain peaks as tall black horns, claiming you could make out two slanted eyes, a sharp nose, and mangled teeth in the rocky façade. Over time, weathering and erosion had changed the landscape, and now, all signs of the demon face were long gone. So far, she hadn't been able to find any photos of the original demon face online, but minus that, the lake before her looked exactly like all the pictures on Google.

There were a few smooth, round stones scattered all around the dock. Picking one up, she tried to skim it across the water. The first attempt was a total failure, but the second one worked, the rock making two skips before it finally sunk. Quickly bored with the game, she brushed herself off and walked back down the dock. She was about halfway to shore when she heard a loud gurgling sound coming from the water behind her. She turned around to see a dark hole forming in the water, right where the second rock had sunk. The water was spinning in a violent circle that kept gaining momentum. Frozen, she watched in horror as the hole grew wide, turning into a gigantic churning vortex. As she stared into the gaping hole, an overwhelming urge to jump in surged through her. Her legs moved on their own volition, taking her back down the dock, closer to the water. She was almost to the edge when a huge wave splashed over the side, soaking her from head to toe. The cold water snapped her back to reality, and she stepped away from the edge, shocked that she'd almost jumped in.

Wave after wave pounded over the rickety boards of the dock. Unable to handle the weight of the water, they began to crack and split. Pulse racing, she made a run for it. She was almost to shore when the board under her foot snapped in half. Falling, she grabbed onto the board in front of her that was still intact. Terrified, she tried to focus on a plan. If she could just get back up on the dock, she could make it to shore and call someone for help. Who, she had no idea, but it gave her something to focus on. After taking a deep breath, she tried to swing her body back and forth to gain enough momentum to get her legs back up on the dock, but it didn't work. Another wave hit her hard in the back, and she almost lost her grip. Shaking it off, she tried to inch her way down the board, hand over hand, aiming for the post on her right side. She was almost there when she saw a sight that made every inch of the hair on her head stand up. The waves below her feet had morphed into two huge black-shaped hands, hands that were reaching for her. She could hardly breathe as terror took over. She kicked and bucked, trying to get away from the water hands, but it was no use. They reared up, grabbed her by the waist, and pulled her under the dark, freezing water.

Chapter 10

Ava woke up thrashing, completely tangled up in her sheets. Sitting up, she tried to break free of the cotton cocoon but only managed to fall off the side of the bed in the process. Landing hard on the wood floor, she just laid there on the ground, trying to catch her breath, a total hot mess of girl and sheets. The sensation of drowning was still so intense that she felt desperate for air.

Before she could even blink, her mom came barreling into the room. "Are you hurt, honey? What happened?"

She sat up again, still wrapped up in the sheets. "I'm fine! I just fell off the stupid bed."

Pausing for a moment to fight with the sheet yet again, she added, "Did Dad tell you about the bad dream I had last night? Well, I just had another one, and it was so much worse! I woke up feeling frantic and somehow fell off the bed!"

Her mom sat next to her on the floor and grabbed her hands, but Ava jerked hers back. All she could picture were those watery hands grabbing onto her, and she didn't want anyone touching her at the moment.

Her mom's expression turned from surprise to concern. "Are you sure all this is about bad dreams? Or did something else happen that you're not telling me about? You know you can talk to me about anything, right?"

"No, why would you......"

She quickly realized that her mom might be imagining a thousand horrible things based on her reaction to being touched. "Oh, Mom! No! Nothing bad happened to me! I promise! These dreams are just super intense and freaking me out!"

Her mom's expression was pained, and she felt the need to explain it further to help her understand. "In the dream, there were these black hands that came out of the water and pulled me under. I'm sorry I startled you, but when you touched me, my body just responded in fight mode. I just need a little time to shake it off. Okay?"

Her mom stared at her for a long time, probably contemplating the truth of her story. Then sighing, she nodded in acceptance. "I want to hug you right now, but I'll give you your space."

She smiled, happy that her mom was trying to be understanding for once.

Standing, her mom said, "I don't want to leave you alone, but your dad got called out on a job this morning, and I have to go by the museum for a few hours to get things ready for the exhibit opening next week. I don't know if your dad has his phone on, so if you need anything, call me! I'll keep my cell in my back pocket just in case."

"Mmm-hmmm," she mumbled, still feeling dazed.

Her mom offered a hand, then immediately pulled it back, saying, "Sorry, Sorry!"

She stood on her own, shaking off the sheet that was stuck around her shoulders. As it fell, her mom wrinkled up her nose, "Wow, kid! When was the last time you took a shower?"

Rolling her eyes, she asked, "What are you talking about? I just took one last night!"

"Really? Because you smell like you rolled around in mildew!"

She smelled her hair and almost gagged. "What in the hell?"

Laughing, her mom walked out of the room. "See, I told you! I'd make a shower priority number one today!"

After her mom left, she realized her pajamas smelled moldy as well. She'd just done laundry, even adding extra time on the dry cycle to avoid this very issue. This new house was just full of grossness. First, there were weird smells in her room, and now, the dyer wasn't working right. Great, just great, she thought! After tossing the smelly pajamas into the hamper to be re-washed, she headed inside the adjoining bathroom to clean up. While reaching for her toothbrush out of the medicine cabinet, she caught her reflection in the mirror. There, staring back at her, were two enormous, hand-shaped bruises on both sides of her body. The outline of the fingers stretched upward, wrapping around her back. The marks were in the same spots where the hands had grabbed her in the dream.

Stunned, she dropped the toothbrush. Sinking to the bathroom floor, she slowly rocked herself back and forth. As the steam filled the room, she wondered how long the shower had been running. Five minutes? Thirty? It could have been an hour for all she knew. She had no concept of how long she'd been sitting on the cold tile floor in shock. When she finally mustered up the strength to stand again, the bathroom mirror was fogged over. That was a good thing, she thought. Her mind couldn't process seeing those bruises again right now.

Jumping in the shower confirmed what she already thought. She'd been sitting on the floor for a while; the water was ice cold. She tried to rush through the washing process as fast as she could, but it took several shampoos to get the sour smell out of her hair, and by the time she finished, she was ice cold. Luckily, her robe was hanging on the warming rack by the door. Grabbing it, she headed back to bed, convinced she was still dreaming and would wake up for real later. Sadly, as she lay there staring at the ceiling, reality sank in. She was wide awake. Confused and scared, she didn't know what to do. Did the fall off the bed cause the bruises, she wondered? That didn't seem plausible since they were in the exact spots where the hands had touched her. Or, she thought, maybe she was just losing her mind. The only thing she knew for sure? Sitting and obsessing wasn't going to solve anything. She needed to do something! Anything! The second dream had taken place at Devil's Head Lake, so she thought going there might help her figure some things out. It was a long shot, but grounded or not; she was going to that creepy ass lake with Liv.

Chapter 11

Checking the clock, it was only 10:30 AM. Ava still had plenty of time to get dressed and make it over to Liv's by 11:00 AM. Not knowing what time either of her parents would be homemade sneaking to the lake super risky, but even if she did get caught, what more could they do? It was a risk she was willing to take. Fumbling through her closet, she quickly pulled on thermal pants with a pair of jeans over them. Remembering Liv said it would be even colder at the lake, she grabbed a warm wool sweater and hot hands for the pockets of her jacket. Before walking out the door, she pulled on the last of her cold-weather provisions; a scarf, waterproof boots, and her oversized parka.

On the brief walk to Liv's, her anxiety was on red alert. Worried her dad would drive by and catch her before they even left, she annoyingly rang the doorbell three times in a rush to get out of sight.

Liv opened the door, clearly surprised to see her. "Morning. How'd you get them to let you come?"

Ava walked into the foyer, confused. "How do you know about that?"

Closing the door behind her, Liv said, "I called you twice last night to make sure you were still in. The second time, your mom answered, said you were grounded and told me not to expect a call back anytime soon. I'm guessing taking a day off wasn't okay with them?"

Ava took off her thick parka, hanging it up by the front door. Liv's house was too warm to keep it on, "No, not at all! I mean, I knew they'd be pissed if they found out, but I thought they'd be a little more understanding. Boy, was I wrong!"

Liv sighed, "Don't take this the wrong way. I'm happy you're coming, but are you sure you should?"

She sat down on the soft brown leather sofa and shrugged. "My parents are both working today, so as long as we get back before they do, I should be good."

She loved Liv's house. It was all warm and inviting, the total opposite of her own. It was strange how perception and reality could be vastly different. Ava's house could be filled with people and still feel empty, while Liv's empty house always felt full. When Liv sat down next to her, she debated telling her about the bruises. On the one hand, Liv was a super understanding person, but on the other hand, most of the things that had happened sounded super crazy. Right now, she wasn't sure she could handle the rejection if Liv didn't believe her, so for the time being, she kept her mouth shut.

Liv bumped her shoulder lightly, interrupting her thoughts. "Are you sure you're, okay? You've been staring at the wall for like ten minutes now."

Ava had no idea how ten minutes had already gone by. Faking a yawn, she lied, "Yeah, I'm just exhausted.!"

Liv sighed, "If you don't want to talk about it, it's okay, but you just don't seem like yourself!"

Even though she wasn't ready to tell Liv the whole truth, she still wanted to tell her something. "Really, I'm fine. I just keep having nightmares, and they're messing with my sleep. The one I had last night took place at Devil's Head Lake."

She paused, taking a deep breath, "To make a long story short, I ended up drowning at the end of it, and I've felt super anxious since I woke up this morning. I've never had nightmares before. Maybe the stress from the move is what's causing them. Or maybe all the research I've done on the lake is messing with me. Either way, I'm glad we're going. I just want to see it for myself, and maybe then, the nightmares will stop."

Liv leaned in and gave her a big hug. "I know the past few weeks have been hard on you, but I'm glad your family moved here. I think your right though, I've been a few times, and it's not as creepy as everyone says it is."

Hugging her back, Ava thought, maybe Liv was right. Why risk the wrath of her parents just to visit some stupid lake? At that moment, the universe responded with a loud, blaring horn.

"Gabe's here!" Liv announced, just as the horn beeped again. "And he's obviously got some patience issues today! You ready?"

She was ready. But for what, she didn't quite know. Nodding, Ava grabbed her parka and followed Liv out the front door.

Chapter 12

Gabe's black SUV was half in the street, half in the driveway, making her even more nervous. She'd never driven anywhere with him before, and by the looks of his parking job, his driving skills needed some improvement. Gabe's sister Holly jumped out of the front seat, motioning for Liv to sit up front next to Gabe. After she climbed into the back with Holly, Gabe turned up the volume to a ridiculous level, assaulting their ears with the annoying sound of dubstep.

Covering her ears, she yelled over the music. "Dude!! Do you mind turning that down before I go deaf?"

Gabe turned around and smiled at her. "What? Not a fan of Bassnectar?"

He was wearing his usual outfit, a black t-shirt with an XMEN logo and faded black jeans.

"Please! You know you're the only one that likes that crap!" Holly yelled.

Holly and Gabe were total opposites in looks and personality. If Liv hadn't told her they were related, she never would have guessed it. Holly was a petite blonde with an affinity for fashion and a guru in all forms of social media. While dark-haired Gabe preferred the just rolled out of bed look and couldn't care less about anything he didn't read in a comic book.

Gabe turned around in his seat, pointing at Holly.

"You wouldn't know good music if it slapped you in the face. Who's your flavor of the week this week, Lady Gaga?"

Instead of answering him, Holly just stuck her tongue out. Today, she wore a tight, long-sleeved sweater, covered by a puffy vest, and skinny jeans paired with three-inch-high boots. Holly looked more ready for a night out on the town than a picnic by the lake. But to each their own, she thought.

"I didn't know you were coming today, but it's a nice surprise!" Ava said.

Holly smiled. "Thanks. To be honest, I didn't really want to come. But Gabe's been nagging me all week, and I finally caved!"

Gesturing towards Liv in the front seat, she said, "Yeah, I know the feeling!"

Holly leaned in and whispered, "You know he has a huge crush on her, right? That's the only reason I agreed to come. I like Liv, and I don't want him messing it up! Honestly, I have no idea why he wants me to go to the lake when he knows I hate it and…."

Holly's voice trailed off, as she nervously wrung her hands together.

Ava didn't want to pry but considering why she was on this trip in the first place; curiosity got the best of her. "I know it's none of my business, and we don't know each other very well, but for me, sometimes talking about what's bothering me helps. If you need to vent, I'm a good listener."

"Thanks!" Holly said hesitantly, but instead of elaborating, she just stared out the window.

Disappointed, she looked out her window and started counting the barren trees to pass the time. She had just reached twenty-six when Holly blurted out, "I'm freaking out! I haven't been back to the lake since I was younger. You know, when the whole Kade thing happened. Gabe thinks I have a little PTSD or something and swears going back will help me cope. I don't think it will, and I have no idea how he can handle it!"

She knew that Kade was one of the kids that had gone missing at the lake from overhearing Adam and Gabe argue about him. Plus, his name had come up in a lot of the research she'd done on the lake. Unfortunately, all the articles she'd come across had been short and to the point. Aside from the names of the missing people and dates, no other descriptions or statements had been available online.

"I'm so sorry, Holly. Maybe Gabe's right. But if not, we're all here for you, and I'm fine with leaving if you need to."

Holly smiled a little and stopped fidgeting.

Ava knew she might be pushing too hard, but she just had to know the whole story. Crossing her fingers that Holly wouldn't freak out, even more, she went for it.

"Holly, I know it's a difficult topic, but do you mind telling me exactly what happened? I've heard bits and pieces from Gabe and Adam but never wanted to pry.

Honestly, I feel horrible prying now! So, if you don't want to talk about it, I understand. No pressure!"

Holly nodded. "It's okay. I'll tell you my version of the story, but no one except for Gabe believes it. Not to sound rude or anything, but I don't care if you do either. I know what I saw!"

"Fair enough!" Ava said, pivoting around in her seat to give Holly her full attention. The music was still loud enough that Gabe and Liv couldn't hear them from the front seats.

"When I was ten, our parents took us to Devil's Head Lake for a big camping trip. Adam and Kade came with us. Growing up, our families were close, and we took a lot of summer trips together. Anyway, it was our last night, and I was pissed off at Gabe because he hadn't found time to take me fishing. After dinner, we got in a huge fight about it, and our parents split us up. The boys slept in the SUV, and I got one of the tents. Later, after everyone fell asleep, Kade snuck into my tent and offered to take me out to the dock for a quick fishing lesson. He was always nice like that."

Holly paused for a moment, nervously tucking her hair behind her ears. "Our campsite was a little way from the lake, so we grabbed two lanterns, all the fishing gear we could carry, and headed out. When we reached the dock, the full moon was so bright that we barely needed the lanterns. We set up the poles, and then he taught me how to bait the hook and cast the line. After that, it took almost an hour before I got my first bite. I tried my best to reel the fish in on my own, but the sucker put up a huge fight. After one big tug that almost pulled me off the dock, Kade took over. He strained and tugged, but the thing wouldn't budge. At one point, the pole bent so far over; I swore it was going to snap in half. Kade kept wrestling with it, joking that I must have caught the Loch Ness

Monster. While he was struggling, I started hearing these horrible growling sounds coming from all around us. After that, everything else happened so fast, and it's hard to remember it all clearly."

Tears began rolling down her cheek just as Gabe spoke up, "It's alright, Holls. If you need to take a break, I'll tell her the rest later."

Lost in the story, she hadn't even noticed when Gabe turned down the music.

"No, no, Gabe. I'm okay. It's just so sad." Holly's bottom lip trembled as she wiped her eyes. "Like I was saying, it all happened so fast. Kade was still struggling with the fishing pole, not aware of the strange noises. I was only a few feet away from him, so I have no idea how he didn't hear them. Scared, I reached out and tapped him on the shoulder. When he turned around, the fishing pole slipped out of his hand and sank into the lake. When it did, the water started bubbling up around the same area, and then out of nowhere, a big crater opened in the lake. Kade was still facing me, so he didn't see the two black hands reaching out of the water. I didn't have time to warn him or even get a sound out of my mouth. Before I could even blink, those horrible hands grabbed onto him and pulled him off the dock. He screamed once and then disappeared! I ran to the edge but couldn't see him in the water. The hole disappeared before my eyes, and the lake looked completely normal again. I just stood there, too terrified to jump in after him. It's all my fault!"

The last words came out as a sob, as Holly broke down completely. Gabe was talking, probably trying to comfort her, but Ava couldn't hear him over the pounding of her own heart. Her stomach pitched, and a sheen of sweat broke out all over her skin. Swallowing hard to keep from vomiting, she stared at Holly in shock. What the girl had just described was an exact play-by-play of her dream.

At some point, Holly had begun speaking again, so she tried to focus. "I ran back to camp as fast as I could and woke everyone up screaming! My mom called 911 while all the boys swam out in the lake to look for him. When the police arrived, I told them exactly what happened, but of course, they didn't believe me. Everyone thinks he drowned, and I made it all up out of shock or guilt!"

Ava squeezed Holly's hand, unsure of what else to do. At the moment, she was having a mental meltdown of her own and was incapable of helping Holly process anything. After Holly composed herself, no one else spoke for the rest of the drive, and she was grateful for the hour of silence. As they got closer to the lake, she wondered how Holly could have seen the same thing in real life that she'd experienced in a dream. Terrified that her dream might be some prolific message, Ava seriously regretted taking this trip.

Chapter 13

Ava snapped back into reality just as the SUV rolled to a stop. For the past hour, she'd been lost inside her mind, obsessing over every unanswered question. So much so that she hadn't even realized they were approaching the lake. The parking area was just a big dirt path a few yards from the lake. Looking out the window, she noticed a few other cars parked nearby. For some reason, she felt better knowing other people were around. Cautiously, she opened the door, slowly sliding out of the backseat. Liv was still sitting in the front, rummaging through her purse, when she knocked on the window, causing Gabe to sputter in protest.

"Oh, no, you don't!" he yelled, quickly beating feet around to their side of the car to open the door for Liv. Dumbstruck, Liv just sat there staring at him.

After a few uncomfortable seconds, Gabe finally said, "Oh, come on! Let me at least attempt to be a gentleman, will you?" Liv smiled hesitantly but took his hand.

Despite all the craziness going on in her head, she had to bite back a laugh. Gabe was making his intentions clear, and Liv was so not on board. Holly shouted a loud "whoop" as she jumped out of the back seat. Talk about making an uncomfortable situation worse. How did Holly think she was helping Gabe with that kind of crap? Holly was as clueless as Gabe was when it came to dating. Then again, she didn't have any knowledge to contribute either.

After they all got out, Gabe and Liv started unloading the picnic supplies. As Liv pulled out a small cooler, she pointed to the car next to theirs. "Looks like Haven's here; that's her Prius."

It didn't escape her attention that Haven's car had a large, black, triquetra decal stuck on the bumper. Grabbing a few bags of supplies, she wondered if today would be the day they finally had a real conversation.

As they walked towards the lake, the sun was shining brightly, and the water was a beautiful clear blue, reflecting the mountains around it. It was everything the internet had depicted and nothing like the end of her most recent nightmare. That comforted her a little. She saw Haven and two other kids sitting around a small fire near the shore as they got closer.

Liv leaned in, whispering, "The boy sitting next to Haven is her cousin. But I don't know the girl."

As soon as Haven recognized them, she waved them over-enthusiastically. "Hey, guys. I didn't know you were coming out today. Want to sit with us? It's already nice and warm."

Haven was wearing her typical all-black attire; a black sweater, black tights, a long black trench coat, all topped off with heavy black eyeliner. Somehow even decked out in the goth style, she was still gorgeous, with her big green eyes and coppery red hair that curled around her shoulders.

Liv pulled a few fleece blankets from her bag and handed one to her before sitting down. Thankful for the extra warmth, she laid the blanket across her lap. Thanks to her extra layer of clothing, the warm fire, and the thick, cozy blanket, she was surprised to find the icy weather almost bearable. Almost!

Haven introduced everyone to her cousin Tuck and his girlfriend, Julie, who attended a Charter School in Colorado and were way into multipurpose art. After the introduction was over, they took off, walking hand and hand down towards the dock. Gabe jumped up, and grabbed Liv by the arm, and followed behind them. Liv let it happen, but Ava could hear her complaining as they walked away. She was semi-warm for the moment and not quite ready to get close to the water. Every time she looked at the lake, the haunting image of those phantom hands played through her mind. Staying put, she looked over at Holly. She seemed to be doing alright for the moment. But then again, it was easy to mask your real feelings if you wanted to. Case in point, she was acting normal when inside her mind was whirling.

"So far, so good, Holly?" she asked.

Holly mumbled an unintelligible response while staring down at the ground. The poor girl couldn't even look at the lake.

Haven overheard their conversation and chimed in, "This is the first time you've been back, isn't it?"

"Yup," Holly answered, her voice barely above a whisper.

"Oh, man! I'm not sure what to say. I mean, my first time back didn't go so well. I drank a bunch of Tito's for liquid courage and threw up in the bushes for like two hours. I don't recommend doing that!"

Holly smiled. "I think you just inspired me to avoid trying hard liquor, so thank you?? But really, how can you stand being here?"

Haven shrugged. "I won't lie to you; it was hard at first, But it's been years now, and I've processed it as best I can.

Despite what happened, I love this place, and I try not to focus on the bad stuff when I'm here."

Holly stood up all hints of a smile now gone. "I'm happy for you, I am, but time just isn't working as well for me. If you guys will excuse me, I want to go talk to Gabe."

"Okay!" Ava and Haven said in unison. Once Holly was gone, Haven pulled out some supplies from her bag and started making s'mores.

"You leave, you lose. Want one?" Haven asked.

"Sure!" she replied, greedily taking the stick from her hand. Excited, she stuck it into the fire and waited impatiently for the marshmallow to melt. Somehow, chocolate always made her feel better about life.

They both sat quietly, nibbling on the s'mores until she decided to break the ice. "It's been a bizarre day, but the chocolate is making everything look shiny again!"

Haven laughed. "Of course, it is. Didn't you know chocolate heals all wounds!?"

Even mental ones? She wondered but didn't dare ask it. Instead, her thoughts drifted back to Holly. She wasn't sure if she should check on her or give her some space.

"I'm sure she's fine," Haven said, "She just needs a little time with her brother. Losing a friend is hard, and they still have a lot of healing to do."

Ava didn't realize she'd spoken aloud until Haven responded. In fact, Ava knew she hadn't. Haven was staring into the fire, seemingly oblivious to the fact that she'd just plucked a thought right out of her head. Holy shit! She thought. Maybe the witch thing was legit. Or maybe, just maybe, she was having another insane moment and had spoken aloud after all. At this point, she didn't have a tight grip on reality, so either could be true. Stuck alone with Haven, she didn't know what to do. She hardly knew the girl and didn't feel comfortable straight up asking her if she was a mind reader. Ava didn't like to admit it, but a small part of her cared what other people thought. She knew she shouldn't care, especially since Haven was practically a stranger, but she couldn't help it.

In an effort to change the subject, she asked Haven a stupid question. "So, um, were you and Kade close?"

Haven sighed. "Very. He was my first boyfriend."

And you lost him, Ava thought. Wow, not only was it a dumb question but an insensitive one. "I'm sorry for prying; that was super rude of me!"

Haven smiled. "Really, it's okay. I don't mind talking about him. He was a fantastic guy, and I want to remember him. Thirteen-year-old me took one look at him and fell head over heels. His eyes were just so amazingly green. They put mine to shame. I've never met anyone else with eyes quite like his, and to be honest, I hope I never do. I want to forever associate them with him. Luckily for me, he ended up being just as beautiful on the inside as he was on the outside."

A picture of the green-eyed boy flashed through her mind, and she got a weird feeling in the pit of her stomach. It felt a lot like déjà vu. It was just an odd coincidence that Kade fit the description of the boy she'd seen at school. Still, something about the dreamy way Haven described his eyes made her feel strange. The next thing she knew, Haven was shaking her arm.

"Earth to Ava! Hello...."

She must have blanked out again. "Yeah, sorry. I'm listening. I just haven't slept much in the past few days and keep zoning out."

Haven was still holding onto her arm tightly. "Haven, I'm good; you can let go now!"

Haven didn't respond. She just sat there, frozen. Trying to shake her off, Ava watched in horror as Haven's eyes filled up with a milky-looking liquid before turning completely white. Then, in a raspy voice that sounded inhuman, she whispered, "The souls are coming for you. Time is running out!"

Adrenaline pumping, she grabbed Haven's hand and ripped it off her arm. Once free, she crab-walked backward across the blanket to get away from her. The second they broke contact Haven's eyes went back to normal. Terrified, Ava sat on the edge of the blanket, panting.

"Why are you looking at me like that?" Haven asked, sounding offended.

Once again, Haven was acting as if nothing effing crazy had just happened. This time, Ava couldn't contain her mouth. "You just went all crazy-eyed and wouldn't let go of me. I don't know how else to look at you. You're freaking me the hell out!"

Haven stared back at her, looking perplexed. "What are you talking about? One minute, you were staring off into space, and the next, you were hustling away from me like I have the plague or something."

Or something indeed, she thought. Haven was genuinely oblivious to what had just occurred, or she was a really good actress. Then again, if Ava was going crazy, maybe she imagined it all. Confused, all she wanted was to get far away from Haven.

Trying to stay calm, she said, "I didn't mean to offend you. As I said, I haven't been getting much sleep lately, and I think I'm starting to have waking dreams or something, You know, like when you doze off for a minute and don't realize it."

Annoyed with the whole situation, Haven snapped back, "Then maybe you should go back home and rest, instead of being rude to people!"

The harsh words hurt even though she agreed with her. Being here was making everything worse! Standing up, she said, "You're right. I'm going to go get the guys and see if they're ready to leave."

"I really do hope you feel better!" Haven said, still sounding annoyed.

Scared and fighting back the tears, Ava beelined it for Liv. She felt like she couldn't talk to anyone about what was happening and just wanted to go home, hide under her blankets, and never come out. When Ava reached the dock, Liv was in the middle of talking to Julie. Not wanting to interrupt, she pulled out her cell phone and pretended to be texting. As she waited, her anxiety rose to a full-on panic attack. Unable to contain it, she bent over, throwing up in the bushes. No Tito's required.

Liv heard her retching and ran over. "Hey. Oh Wow! That's gross! Are you alright?"

"No!" she said, a little too sharply. What to say? What to say? she pondered. Somehow, she had to persuade her friends to drive back to town after being at the lake for less time than it took to get here in the first place. Suddenly, the perfect lie popped into her head.

"My mom just texted me that she's on her way home! I have no idea how she got out early, but we need to go. I'm a nervous wreck, and all the s'mores I ate just backfired on me! I'm so sorry, but can we please go? Now!"

Even though she hated lying to her, it was the only sure-fire way to get them in the car. She knew Liv wouldn't want her to get in any more trouble.

"Oh crap! Of course! Just give me a second to wrangle Gabe and Holly. They headed over that way to talk," Liv said, pointing to a trail on the right side of the lake.

Ava grabbed Liv, hugging the crap out of her. "I owe you big time! Huge!"

"No worries. Gabe might be a little annoyed, but he'll get over it. Hey, maybe you should sit down while I get them. You look a little pale."

Shrugging, Ava said, "I didn't eat breakfast this morning and just threw up the only food in my stomach."

Liv ran off, yelling, "I'll be quick. Go wait by the car while I track them down."

Complying, she hustled towards the SUV, being careful to avoid Haven along the way. Once she reached the car, she walked around to the side facing away from the lake and slumped down to the ground. Feeling like she might hyperventilate, she put her head in her hands and tried to breathe in and out evenly. Five minutes later, the troops arrived.

Before loading up the car, Liv handed her a sandwich, "Please eat this. You don't look well."

Ava had no appetite but took a few small bites of the sandwich to appease her friend. Once everything was packed, Gabe hit the road, driving like a speed demon. Since her lie was the reason for the speeding, she couldn't tell him to slow down. Instead, she prayed they wouldn't get into an accident. On the ride back, no one seemed particularly annoyed with her, and thanks to Gabe's crazy driving, they made it back in half the usual time. When the SUV finally pulled to a stop in her driveway, she jumped out, apologizing to everyone again.

Chapter 14

Stuck alone in the house, Ava couldn't escape her obsessive thoughts. She wanted to believe her dreams and Haven's "possession" had nothing to do with one another, but there was no way it was all just random. Seventeen years of life and not a blip of weird until two days ago. Now, she was smack dab in the middle of a series of paranormal activities. If Haven's white-eyed stint was a common occurrence, then she wondered why that information hadn't made it to the rumor mill. Then again, maybe it had happened to someone else, and they were too scared to tell anyone. It was all just speculation, but that stupid lake was the only common denominator on her train to crazy town.

Her mind was still reeling, even though her body was ready to shut down. The stress and lack of sleep were taking a toll. In the past, the numbness of sleep had always helped calm her overactive mind. Now, she wished for that kind of break but refused to nap, too terrified of what dreams might come. Instead, she paced around her room, trying to work off some anxiety. After half an hour with no relief, she contemplated making coffee but quickly decided against it. Most of the time, caffeine exacerbated her anxiety symptoms, and they were already on red alert. What she needed was to get her blood pumping, but it was too cold outside for a run. Running was her frenemy. She hated it but always felt amazing after a good 5k. With limited options, she decided to try out the treadmill in her parent's room.

The master bedroom had a sleeping area and a separate sitting area that her mom turned into a home gym. Since neither of her parents had time to hit a real gym, this helped them stay fit. The home set up had; a pull-out treadmill, small weight rack, bookshelf full of workout and yoga DVDs, and a mini-fridge stocked with bottled water. The flat-screen T.V. in the corner hung on a swivel mount, so her parents could watch T.V. in bed or turn it to face the gym area. She skimmed over the rack of DVDs and decided to try a circuit training video instead of hitting the treadmill. After an hour of lunges, squats, and high-intensity cardio intervals, she wanted to die. Completely out of breath, she sat down on the floor and chugged an entire bottle of water. If she learned anything today, it was that she was entirely out of shape. New life goals: don't go insane and drop it like a squat more often.

Done, for the time being, she put away the DVD and walked into her parent's bathroom to grab a towel. She wet it under the sink and used it to wipe the sweat off her face and neck. Sitting on the counter, next to her mom's makeup, was an orange pill bottle. She picked it up and read the label. Ambien. A quick google search on her phone confirmed they were sleeping pills. Setting the bottle down, she headed back to her room, intending to take a shower, but just as she stepped into the hallway, a thought crossed her mind. If she took a sleeping pill, would she still dream? She didn't know the answer, but she was desperate for rest, the temporary high from the workout already fading to fatigue. Conflicted, she walked back into the bathroom, picked up the pill bottle, and read the instructions: Take one pill at bedtime to promote healthy sleep.

That sounded easy enough. Decision made, Ava filled up her empty water bottle in the sink, downed the pill, and prayed her plan worked. Not wanting to see the horrible bruises on her sides again, she opted to skip the shower. Instead, Ava changed out of her sweat-soaked clothes, washed off with a washcloth, and put on a clean pair of pajamas. Settling into bed, she noticed it was just after three in the afternoon. Attempting to kill time until the Ambien kicked it, she grabbed her book and picked up where she'd left off the day before. After reading two chapters, her head began to feel heavy, the words on the page blurring. Excited by the prospect of dreamless sleep, she set the book down on her nightstand and closed her eyes.

Chapter 15

When Ava opened her eyes, she found herself lying on a massive four-poster bed in a foreign room, covered in sweat. It was so hot she could see the heat waves rippling through the air. On top of being sweltering, the smell of rotten eggs was overwhelming. Sitting up, she wiped the sweat off her forehead and continued to look around in confusion. The room was round, with a high soaring ceiling, but it had no windows. The walls were made of brick, while the floor and ceiling were carved from a smooth gray stone. There were two oversized chairs on the opposite side of the room that faced a massive stone fireplace. She swung her feet over the side of the bed, but before they reached the floor, a familiar voice spoke up.

"There's no need to get out of the bed. You won't be here long."

Startled, she snapped her head in the direction of the voice but didn't see anyone at first. Slowly, a tall figure stood up from one of the chairs, and when he turned around, his green eyes confirmed what she already knew.

"You again!" she yelled! "What's going on? Where am I?" Panicked, she shot off question after question.

He stepped towards her, a cocky grin on his face. "I told you to stay on the bed!"

"I don't care what you said. Stay over there!"

He stopped walking, all humor in his eyes fading. "Ava, calm down. I will answer all your questions, but right now, you need to listen. We don't have much time."

"Time? Time for what?? God, why is it so hot in here, and what is that horrible smell? I swear it's following me!" she said, sweat dripping off her forehead.

His stare turned to concern. "That smell is sulfur. When exactly did you smell it before?"

The heat was making her feel woozy. "I don't remember…wait, it was Friday, the day I skipped school. I smelled it in my bedroom. Right, right after I had a dream about you!"

"Friday?" he growled.

"Yes! Friday! Wait, I'm getting distracted. A stupid smell is not what's important right now. Where the hell are we?"

Aggravated, she grabbed the edge of the bedsheet and used it to wipe the sweat off her face.

He didn't answer her again but seemed to soften a bit. "My apologies, I'm used to the heat. This should help a little."

Lifting his right hand, he shot a massive ball of bright blue light across the room. The light landed in the fireplace, erupting in blue dancing flames. Fascinated by what she'd witnessed, all her previous questions were forgotten.

"How did you do that?" she asked in awe.

Avoiding her questions for the third time, he said, "I know strange things have been happening to you, but it will all make sense soon."

Rolling her eyes, she said, "Really? Because I don't think it will. I think all of this is just me losing my god damn mind!"

He shook his head, taking a few steps toward her again. "Your mind is very sound."

As he moved closer, she scooted backward. "Please don't fear me. I would never hurt you." he said with a sigh.

She kept scooting until her back was pressed firmly against the headboard. "I don't even know you! Why should I trust you?"

He sat down next to her, taking her hand in his. On contact, she felt a warm sensation rush up her arm. Startled, she tried to pull her hand away, but he held on tightly. She looked down at where their hands were joined, then back up to his face. He seemed so innocent, his bright green eyes practically begging for her trust. Seeming satisfied, he let go of her hand. "You said you dreamed about me the other night and smelled sulfur when you woke up. Has anything else you dreamed about manifested in real life?"

Nodding, she pulled up the side of her shirt, showing him one of the dark purple bruises marring her side.

He cursed under his breath, "It's worse than I thought! Others are coming for you, and I need to make sure you're protected. Can you do something for me?"

"What do you mean, others?" she was over this cryptic bullshit.

"So many weird things have happened to me over the last few days, and now you're telling me that people are coming after me? Why?? Why me? No! You know what, don't' even bother answering. It doesn't matter! This is just another stupid dream! And nothing you say is real!"

He grabbed her hand again, this time bringing it up to his lips for a soft kiss. Her stomach dropped when his lips touched her skin.

"Believe it or not," he whispered, "This is real. And if you want proof, I need you to meet me at Devil's Head Lake on Monday. Please, Ava, promise me you will?"

He asked with such conviction that she felt compelled to accept. Then he took her face in both his hands, angling her head, so she was forced to stare directly into his eyes. Eyes that were suddenly so bright they were glowing. Mesmerized, her body felt weightless. As she continued to drift, the green in his eyes slowly faded until nothing was left but a black void.

Chapter 16

Ava awoke to her mom's sing-song voice, "Good Morning, birthday girl, it's time to get up!"

Morning? How was it morning already, she wondered. Cracking her eyelids open, she watched as her mom flutter around the room like a hummingbird, opening all the curtains to let in the morning light. In response, she cringed, pulling the covers back over her head. That Ambien was no joke, she thought. It had knocked her out for a good seventeen hours, but somehow, even inside her sleep-induced coma, she still remembered the dream about the green-eyed boy. At least this latest dream hadn't been scary like all the others. After being knocked out for almost an entire day and still dreaming, she officially considered the Ambien test a failure vowing never to try it again. It was time to find a real solution to her problems and not just a Band-Aid.

Peeking out from underneath the covers, she glared at her mom. "You are way too perky this morning!!!"

Her mom smiled teasingly while pulling off her blankets. Ava was immediately assaulted with bright light and cold air. "Hey, you give that back!"

"No way, lady! Your Dad and I made sure we were both off for your birthday. We can do anything you want, so let's get up and get moving!"

"What if the only thing I want to do is sleep?" she asked mockingly.

"Seriously?" her mom asked. "You just slept for almost an entire day!"

Defeated, Ava sat up in bed. "I know, but it was catch-up sleep. The past few nights have been rough."

Her mom was still bustling around the room, straightening things that were already perfect, when she came across the novel Ava was reading.

Picking it up, her mom rolled her eyes before placing it back down. "You read all that weird paranormal stuff and then wonder why you have bad dreams. Maybe it's time to switch to another genre!"

"Mom, those books aren't even scary! Plus, I've been reading them for years and never had nightmares until now. These dreams are horrible and nothing like my books!"

"If you say so, but I'm just trying to help! Did you have any nightmares during your marathon of sleep last night?"

Annoyed her mom was downplaying the whole thing, she harshly blurted out, "No! Lucky me!"

Her mom missed the tone in her voice. "Well, good! Now, back to the plans. Any idea what you'd like to do?"

While she was impressed both her parents had managed to get the day off, the idea of hanging out with them for an entire day felt a little intimidating. What to do, what to do, she wondered. The first thing that popped into her mind was sushi. She hadn't had any since they left Florida, and just the thought of a spicy tuna roll had her mouth-watering.

"How about sushi and shopping?" she suggested.

"It's your day. If that will make you happy, then that's what we will do. I can't guarantee your dad will enjoy the shopping part, though. There are a few good sushi places by my museum in Denver. Why don't you get ready and we can leave in thirty? Sound good?"

"Perfect! Thanks, Mom!"

Three hours later, she was full of sushi and happier than she'd been in a long time. The drive to Denver had been pleasant, with lots of uninterrupted conversation, and she was thankful that neither of her parents had brought up the skipping issue. So far, it was turning out to be a decent birthday. Before today, she hadn't given much thought to turning eighteen. Legally, she was an adult. While, technically, she was still a child. She didn't have a job or a car and still lived at home; none of those equaled adulting.

After lunch, her dad left them at the mall, claiming he had some "manly" errands to run. Her mom then proceeded to drag her from store to store, looking at shoe after shoe, until she was bored out of her ever-loving mind. Her idea of shopping was hitting one store, not an entire mall. But even though this wasn't her bag, pun intended, she went along without complaint. She didn't get much, scratch that, any quality time with her mom, and she was trying hard to appreciate it, despite the sore feet. After leaving what felt like the hundredth store, they stopped in a Starbucks for a quick recharge. When they walked inside, her mom immediately made eye contact with a short blonde woman sitting alone by the window. Waving in the women's direction, her mom whispered, that's my friend Sharon. You remember me talking about her, right? She works at the museum with me."

Ava didn't remember hearing anything about the women, but she decided to nod and play along since they were having such a nice day.

Sharon walked up, giving her mom a big hug. "Lynne, it's so good to see you outside of the gallery! Oh, my goodness, this must be your Ava! Hi, I'm Sharon! It's so nice to meet you finally!"

"Likewise!" she said with a fake smile.

"It's such a coincidence running into you both today. Julie was just telling me how much she enjoyed meeting you yesterday at the lake."

Her mom's head snapped in her direction, just as her heart dropped into her stomach. In a way too sweet tone, her mom then asked, "What is she talking about, honey? Haven't you been grounded since Friday?"

Caught red-handed, she couldn't think of a good excuse on the spot. Instead, she just stood there, staring at her mom in shock.

"Cat got your tongue?" her mom asked sarcastically.

Sharon looked at her with sympathy. "I didn't mean to cause any problems. If you'll excuse me, I can see that you two have a lot to talk about."

Her mom spoke to Sharon, but kept her eyes fixed on her the entire time. "Really, it's no problem at all, Sharon. Thank you for enlightening me. See you at work tomorrow."

Defeated, poor Sharon headed off in the opposite direction, leaving her alone with one very pissed-off Mom.

"What is going on with you? First, you skip school. Now, you're sneaking out when you're supposed to be grounded?"

Shaking her head, she added, "This is not the daughter I raised!"

Hearing her mom use the word "raised" set her off, "Raised! Raised?! How can you raise someone when you're never around?! I missed one day of school, and now I'm not the daughter you knew! Whatever! You and Dad are both ridiculous! I disagreed with your stupid punishment, so I kept my plans with Liv and went to the lake anyway!"

She had never talked back to either of her parents before, and her mom looked genuinely shocked over the outburst.

"How dare you be so disrespectful! Forget the coffee. We're going home! NOW!"

"Fine!" she yelled back.

As they walked towards the exit, all the people in the coffee shop turned back around, pretending they hadn't just been watching their argument. They stood outside in silence for a good twenty minutes until her dad finally pulled up at the curb. The drive back to Fox Field sucked, big time! Her mom relayed the entire story to her dad, who just kept looking at her in the rearview mirror, shaking his head. She didn't care if they were disappointed, she knew she was a good kid, and a one-time, okay, two-time mess up wasn't the end of the world.

Ava waited until her mom finished talking and then asked, "How does Julie even know I'm your daughter?"

Her mom turned around, shooting her a look of death, "Sharon is Julie's Mom. Sharon and I share an office at work, and I have pictures of you all over my desk. Julie's school is right down the street from the museum, so she comes by a few times a week to ride home with Sharon. She must have recognized you from my pictures."

That made sense, but she wondered why Julie hadn't mentioned it at the lake. Maybe she hadn't made the connection until later. Then again, she hadn't had much time to talk to Julie before she rushed everyone back to town.

When they finally made it home, she bee-lined it for her room, but her dad stopped her, yelling, "Where do you think you're going? We're not done!"

Annoyed, Ava turned around and walked back into the living room, mentally preparing for the very long lecture. She hadn't even made it to the couch before her dad started in on her.

"I don't know what's gotten into you, but it's going to stop. Right now! Do you think being eighteen means you no longer have to follow the rules? If so, you're seriously mistaken!"

She couldn't help but backtalk him. "I wasn't eighteen when I skipped school or went to the lake."

He ignored her comment and kept on with his tirade. "If you miss one more day of school or lie to us in any way, you can kiss all your privileges goodbye for the rest of senior year!"

"Dad, I get it. Alright! But, don't you think you're going a little overboard?"

"No, young lady, I don't! And since you keep mouthing off, you're grounded for the entire week!"

"Seriously? Look, I'm sorry! You're right about the lake. It was wrong to sneak around, and I won't do anything like that again. Will you please reconsider?"

Frustrated, he paced back and forth for a few minutes before responding. "No! One whole week! I want to make sure the point hits home!"

"I hate you sometimes!" she said, immediately regretting it.

He sighed. "You can hate me all you want, but you will respect my rules. Now go to your room!"

"Gladly!" she shouted, tears welling in her eyes.

She was so angry she felt like punching something. Instead, she picked up the book from her bedside table and threw it to the ground. Hard! As it fell, her right palm began to tingle, and a bright white light shot out of it, hitting the book dead center. Awestruck, she walked over to investigate. The front cover of the book was burned, and it felt warm to the touch. Grabbing a pillow off the bed, she threw it in the air, hoping to repeat whatever had just happened. Vexingly, it landed softly on the floor, completely unscathed.

Angry and frustrated, she stomped into the bathroom to take a warm bath. Once the tub was filled to the point of spilling over, Ava sank into the hot water and tried to relax. On a typical day, she would have lost her mind over what had just happened. On day four of the "Ava is delusional tour," it didn't bother her so much. The only logical explanation was that she was having some kind of mental breakdown that caused her to hallucinate and have nightmares. Maybe all the stress from the move was manifesting itself into physical symptoms. The truth was, as the days went by, her situation was continuing to deteriorate. It was time for her to be honest with herself and stop blaming her problems on fantasy. She needed to talk to her parents and see about getting some help, even if that meant seeing a shrink. For the time being, she closed her eyes, attempting to push away all the bad feelings.

She was just getting settled in the tub when she heard whispering coming from somewhere inside the bathroom. Sitting up, she looked around, but nothing was there. Cautiously, she lowered herself back down. As soon as she did, the whispers started up again, louder this time. Jolting upright, she sloshed a ton of water over the side of the tub, but again, no one was there. Great, she thought, just great.

Along with nightmares and hallucinations, she was now hearing voices! The whispers started up again, slowly growing louder until they erupted into a chorus of voices. Scratchy, guttural voices that sounded muffled. They kept talking and talking until she realized they were repeating the exact phrase over and over. Leaning her head outside the tub, she strained to make out the words. Finally, one voice sounded more precise than the others, "You can't escape us!" the voice repeated, over and over.

Then another voice, right by her ear, whispered, "Kade thought he could keep you safe! Stupid boy!"

Suddenly, strands of black smoke swirled up from underneath the bathwater, wrapping themselves around her legs like vines. The smoke continued to climb up her body and torso, finally reaching both of her arms. She tried to stand up, but the smoke constricted around her tightly, making it impossible to move. After they covered her completely, the strands began to twist, digging deeper and deeper into her flesh. Frantically thrashing around in the water, she tried with all her strength to break free. It was useless! The more she struggled, the tighter the strands dug into her skin until finally, it was too much, and she screamed out in pain. An instant later, her dad burst into the bathroom.

"Get it off, get it off!" she cried, still thrashing around in the tub.

"Get what off, honey?!" her dad asked. Frantically, looking her over from head to toe.

"It's all over me!! Please Daddy, please!"

Her dad knelt by the side of the tub, gently placing his hands on her shoulders. "Calm down, baby. You're okay! There's nothing here. Look!"

Confused, she opened her eyes to find that all remnants of the smoke were gone. Even her skin looked normal. Staring into her dad's concerned face, she couldn't hold back the tears. As she sobbed, he hugged her tightly against his chest.

"What happened, Ava?" he asked, gently rubbing her back.

"I must have fallen asleep in the tub." She wasn't sure if that was a lie or the truth.

"These nightmares of yours are getting really out of hand. I think we should take you to see a doctor."

She knew he was right and simply nodded in agreement.

As he helped her stand up, she quickly realized she was completely naked in front of her dad. Mortified, she grabbed the shower curtain and pulled it around her body.

"Umm? Can I have some privacy, please?"

Her dad turned his head. "Sure, honey, I'll just be right outside the door."

After drying off and donning her robe, Ava took a shaky step out of the bathroom to find both of her parents waiting for her. Concerned, they kissed her goodnight and tucked her into bed before leaving the room. She couldn't remember the last time they'd done that. As she lay there, too scared to fall asleep, she nervously laughed at her situation. Instead of getting a new coat this winter this year, she was probably getting a straight jacket. The gossip headline at school would read, "Girl turns eighteen and goes bananas. B-A-N-A-N-A-S!"

Chapter 17

Ava woke up early for school the following day, with one person on her mind. Kade!

In the bathroom the night before, one of the voices had explicitly said, "Kade thought he could keep you safe! Stupid boy!"

At the time, she'd been too terrified to pay much attention to the name. Now, it was all she could think about.

It was Monday, the same daydream boy had asked her to meet him at the lake, but even if she wanted to go, there was no way to get out there. She didn't own a car or have enough money for the extended cab ride. Besides, she thought, it was time to face reality. She was the problem, not something supernatural. A small, strange part of her still wanted to believe everything was real. The truth was, both of her options sucked. Either she was going insane, or paranormal activity existed. Her current goals were: get to school early to find Holly and then somehow sweet-talk her into giving up more information on Kade. For some reason, she felt the need to investigate him before completely accepting her mental fate. If the smoke in the bathroom had been just another hallucination, then nothing would come of it anyway. No harm, no foul, she thought.

Every time she pictured Haven's description of Kade's green eyes, it gave her a weird feeling in the pit of her stomach. That, combined with the fact that some weird voices that may or may not have been a hallucination, had named him specifically, made her curiosity spike off the charts. On the way out, she walked through the front foyer, spying her cell phone lying on the entryway table. It had a note stuck to it that read: For emergencies only, you're still grounded!

Like she needed the reminder. She had a ton of text and voice mail messages from friends, wishing her a happy birthday. Five of them were from Kat alone, ranging from sweet to angry. Kat didn't know she was grounded, and Ava was royally pissed off that she hadn't called her back in days. Ava smiled, thinking about how much she loved Kat. To avoid a potential Kat-strophe later, Ava shot her a quick text message, promising to call her back after school. As she passed Liv's house, she considered stopping but ultimately didn't. Ava felt guilty, but Liv was perceptive, and she couldn't fake meaningless chitchat today. Instead, she sent her a text message as well, explaining that she was going into school early to grab her makeup work and would get her up to speed on everything during second period.

Ava waited outside Holly's classroom for a good twenty minutes, hoping to catch her before class, but the girl never showed. Frustrated, she had no choice but to head on to first period when the bell rang. For the entire hour, she stared at the clock, oblivious to what the teacher was saying. Five minutes before the second bell rang, she excused herself, claiming a bathroom emergency, and bee-lined it back to Holly's classroom. After the second bell rang, student after student filed out into the hallway, but there was still no sign of Holly.

Disappointed, she headed into the bathroom before going on to second period. She was right in the middle of washing her hands when Haven walked in. Great, she thought, could this day get any worse? Haven looked equally excited to see her but still managed a smile.

"Hey Ava, how's it going?" she asked.

Shrugging, she said, "Better. How about you?"

"Can't complain," she answered while walking into an open stall.

Talk about an awkward moment. Drying off her hands as quickly as possible, Ava exited stage left. On her way to class, she passed by the Student Office and finally hit the jackpot. Through the glass wall, Ava spied Holly and Gabe, checking in late at the front desk. Sitting down on the bench outside of the door, she impatiently waited for them to finish. They were in the middle of an argument when they walked out, so Ava didn't want to interrupt. Instead, she followed them down the hallway and waited until Gabe stopped at his locker to tap Holly on the shoulder.

Holly jumped in response. "Oh! Hey Ava, you scared me!"

"I'm sorry. I didn't mean to. I was just wondering if you have a second to talk?" She knew Kade was a touchy subject for Holly and felt bad bringing it back up, "Um, it's about Kade."

Holly walked over to her locker and began shoving books inside. "Sure, what's on your mind?"

Ava leaned up against the locker next to Holly's. "I just need to know if you have a picture of him. This might sound a little weird, but after hearing all the stories about him, I'd like to put a face to the name."

Holly looked at her with pity in her eyes. "I'm not judging you. I mean, I've done and seen my share of weird things, but don't you think it's a little morbid to look at a picture of a dead kid?"

Holly was right, but she still had to know. Trying to play off the sympathy card, she put on her best sad face and shrugged her shoulders in defeat. "Yeah, you're probably right."

The move worked like a charm. Holly sighed and patted her on the shoulder. "Well, we have tons at home, but if you want to see one today, you should just go to the library. The school keeps copies of all the old yearbooks.

Kade attended freshman year, before the accident, so his photo will be in there."

Her pulse began racing, and it took everything in her not to sprint away from Holly towards the library. Somehow, she managed to compose herself long enough to give Holly a quick hug and say, "Thank you!"

"Sure." Holly replied, hugging her back.

She walked away casually until she reached the corner. Then, it was go time. She took off at a dead run, bumping into random students along the way. She got a lot of mean looks and eye rolls but couldn't care less. Plowing through the library's double doors like a tiny tornado, she ran to the front desk to find the librarian. She wasn't there. Deciding to search on her own, it took twenty minutes before she finally found the correct section. The yearbooks were tucked away in a back corner, close to the supply closet. She scanned the bookcase until she found the right year, then slowly slid the book out. It was purple, just like everything else at the school. Sitting, she opened the book, then quickly slammed it shut. No matter what was on the page, she had to know the truth. Heart pounding, she opened it again, quickly scanning the back index to find Kade Richter's name. He was on page nineteen. Slowly, she turned to the correct page.

After looking down, the world as she knew it officially ended. Hands shaking, she lost her grip on the book, and it landed on the ground with a loud thud. There, staring back at her, was the green-eyed boy. It was all real! Kade was somehow reaching out to her from the other side. If he was a ghost, that didn't explain how he'd been corporal the first time she'd seen him, but at this point, nothing made any sense. The bell for third period rang just as she jolted into action. Shaking, she bolted out of the library, heading straight for the lunchroom.

Chapter 18

Ava found Gabe and Megan sitting alone at the table. Good, she thought, the last person she wanted to run into right now was Liv. She walked up to them, rudely interrupting their conversation. It wasn't a very nice thing to do, but these were desperate times. Plus, Megan was rude to everyone, like always, so giving her a dose of her own medicine felt good.

"Gabe, I need to talk to you out in the hall for a minute. It's an emergency!" she was nervous and sweating.

Gabe took one look at her and followed her out into the hall. When they were alone, she bent over, feeling like she might hyperventilate. In response, Gabe patted her lightly on the back.

"Whoa! Are you alright? Need me to call the nurse?"

Ava stood slowly, trying to catch her breath. "No, no, nurse! I know this is a lot to ask, but I need you to drive me to Devil's Head Lake today!"

Gabe smiled. "Okay, no problem! I can drive you there right after school, but what's the emergency?"

"That is the emergency!" she yelled. "I can't wait until after school. I need to go right NOW!"

Gabe's eyes shot open wide, and he took a step away from her. "Look, you're clearly upset about something, and I'm listening, but yelling at me will get you nowhere. Unless you can give me a good reason why I should risk getting in trouble for skipping, I'm not taking you anywhere. Especially since Holly and I were already late this morning."

She decided to just lay it all on him. If he thought she was crazy, then so be it. "Fine. You want honesty!? Here goes, I saw Kade! As in, I saw him in person, Gabe.

He was here at school a few days ago, and I've been dreaming about him since. I wasn't sure it was him until today when I saw his picture in an old yearbook. He's the same person I've been seeing. In my last dream, he asked me to meet him at the lake today. I can't trust anyone else, Gabe! I know you believe Holly, and I do too! Before Holly told me the story about Kade, I had already dreamt about those watery hands. That's why I was acting so weird the other day. I know you think something else happened to all those people. I think you're right. Maybe taking me today will help answer some questions for you. Please help me!!"

Gabe just stood there, staring at her.

"Even if you think I'm insane, just please take me! I'll owe you forever! Please!"

Emotions running high, she couldn't hold back the tears. Gabe pulled her in for a hug.

"Don't cry. I don't know if what you saw was real, but I believe you think it was. No one believed what Holly saw either, and I've seen what that can do to a person, so I'll help you. On one condition."

Hope welled up inside her. "Anything!"

Gabe laughed, "Just put in a good word or twenty for me with Liv."

"Done and done!" she was so happy she could have kissed him.

They made it out of the parking without anyone noticing, and Gabe was quiet for most of the ride, only commenting on silly things, like a funny exit name or billboard. She was thankful he wasn't twenty questioning her since she had zero answers. All she wanted to do was get to the lake and find Kade.

Storm clouds began rolling in over the mountains just as they pulled into the parking area. The thick clouds cast a dark shadow over everything, giving her that weird feeling in the pit of her stomach yet again. The once beautiful blue lake now looked just like the black pit from her nightmare. Gabe parked the car, but she just sat there, not making any moves to get out.

"What now?" he asked as if reading her mind.

"I don't know, just give me a sec."

As they waited, it started to downpour. Peering out through the rain-soaked window, Ava couldn't tell if anyone else was out there. Determined, she opened the door. "I'm going to go down and check it out. You can wait here if you don't want to get wet."

Gabe snorted. "Yeah, right. With all the legends surrounding this place, you don't know what kind of weirdos come out here. You're not going anywhere alone."

Thankful he was here, she tried to fake a reassuring smile. Even though she was acting brave, inside, she was terrified.

"Thanks," she said, jumping out of the car.

By the time they reached the dock, they were both soaked to the bone and freezing. Gabe yelled over the rain. "I don't see anyone. We should just go back and wait in the car for a little while. The weather keeps getting worse."

She could barely hear him over the howling wind but knew he was right. Kade wasn't here. The realization made her chest ache.

Disappointed, she followed Gabe back towards the shore. They were about halfway down the dock when a big gust of wind blew into them, bringing a loud growling sound with it. She looked over at Gabe, and his face had gone completely white.

"What in the hell was that?" he asked, his voice a bit shaky.

Before she had time to answer him, another huge gust knocked them apart. She went flying down the dock, landing near the water's edge, while Gabe ended up in the opposite direction, landing close to the shore. He stood up, immediately running towards her. He looked panicked and yelled something, but she couldn't hear him over the growling noises and howling wind. Gabe was almost to her when something grabbed onto her waist. One second, she was sitting on the dock, and the next, she was under the water. Fighting, Ava kicked and thrashed while the unknown force continued to pull her deeper and deeper under the surface. The last thing she saw before the light faded utterly was the horrified look on Gabe's face as he hung over the side of the dock, reaching for her.

Chapter 19

Whoever said death was peaceful was a big fat liar. It was filled with terror, darkness, and suffocation. Adrenaline pumping, Ava fought with everything she had to reach the surface, but nothing slowed her rapid descent. She knew if she could see through the darkness, she would see those phantom black hands wrapped around her waist. Her dream had somehow come to life, and this time, she was really going to drown. She could only hold her breath for so long, and time was running short. The more she fought, the more her lungs burned. Refusing to give up, she tried to pry the hands off her body manually, but there was nothing to grab on to. She could feel the hands gripping onto her sides, but they had no physical form.

The water pressure became unbearable as she traveled further under, causing her ears to pop and her head to pound. It became impossible to hold her breath any longer, and water forced its way in through her nose. This was it, she thought. She was going to die. With one last burst of strength, she thrashed, kicked, and twisted in a final bid for freedom. When that didn't work, she let out a silent scream under the water, expelling the last bit of air she'd been holding. As if on cue, her body stopped moving, the pressure on her sides dissipating. Panic-stricken, she tried to swim towards the surface, but nothing happened. Floating in place, she could move her arms and legs, but her body didn't go anywhere.

In the distance, she noticed a light blinking in and out. It reminded her of the light she'd seen in the dream about the cave. Without warning, her body shot forward, some unknown force propelling her towards the light. As she moved closer, the light became brighter and brighter until it was blinding. Was she already dead, she wondered? Was this the light that everyone talked about? She no longer felt the need to breathe, and the burning sensation inside her lungs was gone. At barely eighteen, death wasn't something she'd given much thought to. There were so many places she hadn't seen! So many things she still wanted to accomplish! Now, it was all over. Just like that! It was heartbreaking to think of all the people she would never see again; her parents, Kat, Liv, Gabe! Ugh! Poor Gabe! He was probably going to blame himself.

The bright light began to fade, just as the water turned from black to clear. Well, not completely clear, she thought; it had a strange orange tint to it. Looking around, she noticed the bottom of the lake was covered with huge, jagged black rocks that jutted out in every direction. They reminded her of giant sea urchins spread out all over the sand. Out of the corner of her eye, she spotted several black shadows swimming in her direction. Even though she could see through the water, she still couldn't identify what they were from such a long distance. Alarmed by the visitors, she tried to propel her body up towards the surface again.

By some miracle, the second time worked. On the way up, her lungs constricted as the urge to breathe became so intense that she accidentally sucked in a bunch of water. It felt like a lifetime before she finally broke through the water's surface, choking and gasping for air. Treading water, she heaved violently as her body expelled all the water from her lungs. After a lot of slow, choppy breaths, she was finally able to breathe evenly. Unfortunately, that only lasted for about two seconds. As she looked around, the shock of the scenery hit her like a punch to the gut. What she was seeing couldn't be real! Burning black mountains surrounded the lake she was floating in. Red and orange flames licked up the sides of each one, meeting at the top in an explosion of fire. Her eyes followed the fire up to the blood-red sky beyond. A sky that was full of raging grey and black storm clouds. The thick clouds were twisting and rolling together, letting the red- light from the sky filter through. That red light was the cause of the orangish tint to the water. She wondered if she was in Hell, and if so, how had she ended up here? No doubt she had flaws, but overall, she considered herself a decent person.

A large splashing sound pulled her from her thoughts. Unsettled by the landscape, she'd temporarily forgotten about the shadows swimming beneath the water. As she watched in fear, a huge black fin topped with sharp barbs slowly glided across the water's surface. Her first thought was, if I'm already dead, what else can happen to me? Right? Well, if she was indeed dead, it did nothing to ebb her fear. Unsure of what to do, she swam around in a circle looking for somewhere to go. Finally, she spotted a small patch of land near the base of one of the mountains. The fish thing, or whatever it was, crested again, this time, right beside her. As it did, it let out a high-pitched squealing sound that made her cringe. The noise was horrid. Scared, she aimed for the shore, pumping her arms and legs as fast as they could go. Swimming more quickly than she ever thought possible, the creature was still right on her heels. Her fingertips had just brushed up against the rocky bottom when she felt a blinding hot pain lance through her right foot. As the creature bit down, it yanked her back, dragging her away from the safety of the shallow water. Despite the pain, she dug both of her hands into the rocky sand and used her left foot to kick the creature in its face as hard as she could. It let her go, but she knew it was only temporary.

Standing in the shallow water, she tried to run, but her shoes were full of water. Limping in pain, she somehow made it to the shore before the thing came back. The sand was littered with crumbling black rocks, and she only made it a handful of steps before finally falling on her stomach. Exhausted, she rolled over onto her back, trying for the millionth time to catch her breath. The monster was still out in the deeper water, swimming back and forth, stalking her. When its head broke through the surface again, she gasped at the sight of it. It was the size of a small car and looked like a weird cross between a fish and a reptile. It had shiny black scales, beady yellow eyes, and a huge mouth filled with row after row of razor-sharp teeth. The flesh in-between its scales were pink, puckered, and rotting. Her mind couldn't catch up to what her eyes were seeing. It was all too unbelievable and horrifying. Keeping her eyes focused on the water's surface, she scooted backward on her butt, leaving a trail of blood in the sand. Her foot throbbed, but she wanted to put as much distance between her and the water as possible. Once she was at a comfortable distance, she ripped off a piece of her shirt and wrapped it around her foot to help with the bleeding. She had no idea how severe the puncture was but wrapping it up was the best she could do for the moment. Then, as if things couldn't get any worse, she watched in disbelief as all her blood slowly moved through the sand, pooling together into one big puddle. Yes, this was Hell, she thought. No wonder she could still feel pain.

    Looking around, she tried to get her bearings. The small beach stretched out for a few yards in opposite directions, both paths bumping up against the mountains. Walking down either side was out of the question. There was a dense forest located right behind her. She only had two possible options: stay put or enter the forest. Before she had time to decide, another loud splash echoed in the distance. She turned, just in time to see the enormous sea creature flying towards her through the air. With no way of protecting herself, she put her hands up in the air, trying to brace her body from the impact. Closing her eyes, she prayed this was just another terrible dream. Even with her eyelids tightly closed, she still saw the bright flash of light. Then, when nothing else happened, she forced her eyes back open, only to find a massive pile of black ash.

Her palms felt warm, and her entire body was tingling all over. She wondered if she burned it, just like she burned the book in her room. It was the only explanation as to why the creature was gone. Too bad she had no idea how to use it on demand. Without it, she was defenseless here. Here? Where was here? She wondered again. If she was alive, how did she even start to find her way back home? If she was dead, then what was next? She had too many questions and zero answers. Her skin felt like it was already blistering, and the smell of sulfur was making her want to gag. She could sit here on the beach and hope another monster didn't find her or take her chances hiking through the forest with an injured foot. Decision made, she limped towards the forest's edge. Pausing, she glanced back once more, just in time to see the sand open up and swallow her pool of blood. Once every drop was gone, it sifted back into place like nothing happened. Hobbling faster, she entered the sea of lifeless trees, praying this wasn't really Hell.

Chapter 20

The forest was dark, dank, and humid. Luckily, as Ava traveled further inside, the heat from the blazing mountains dissipated to a tolerable level. Coming from Florida, she was used to humidity, the steamy forest feeling just like any other day down South. However, that was where the similarities stopped. None of the red sky was visible through the thick canopy of gnarled tree limbs, and the ground was covered in an eerie blue fog that came right up to her knees. Even though it was dark, thanks to the glow of the weird fog, she could see well enough to maneuver through the trees. She'd never seen trees like these before. They were black, with strange twisting branches that seemed to create sinister shapes in the darkness. Their sparse black leaves were withered, and the trunks oozed a thick red substance that looked a whole lot like blood. She refused to believe it was blood! Not blood, not blood, not blood, she repeated inside her head.

First fish monsters and now bleeding trees! Hell, Hell, Hell, she thought again. For her sanity, she pretended the liquid was gummy berry juice. Yes! Just red, thick, oozing, gummy berry juice. When that didn't work, she tried to focus on happy thoughts. The first one that came to mind was Kat's singing. Closing her eyes, she focused on the sound of Kat's voice, imagining what she might sing in this situation. It would probably go something like, "*Trees and fog, trees and fog, if you don't watch out, you'll trip on a log!*"

Thinking of Kat calmed her down for a few moments until the realization hit that she might never hear her sing again. Overcome with sadness; she walked on for what felt like days, tripping here, scraping herself there. Covered in sweat and dying of thirst, she finally collapsed down on the hard, black dirt, careful not to lean up against any of the trees. Her injured foot was killing her, and she needed a few minutes to rest.

Staring out into the forest, she noticed a small black shadow dart across the path directly in front of her. The fog separated for a second as it passed by, quickly weaving back together. Evil laughter erupted all around the forest, just as more shadows emerged from the darkness. They were circling her, darting in and out of the fog. One passed by right in front of her face, just as searing pain exploded across her right cheek and leg! Reaching up, she touched her face, wincing at the pain. Pulling her hand back, she felt nauseated, seeing it covered with blood. Scared to death, she jumped up, looking down at her leg to assess the damage. Her pants were shredded from the knee down, but lucky, they had taken the brunt of the attack.

Ava wanted to run, but her foot wouldn't cooperate. As she hobbled through the woods, the loud laughter rang again, as another shadow jumped out in front of her. This time, it slashed her twice across the stomach. The pain was so intense, it caused her knees to buckle, and as she fell, the shadows attacked in full force, clawing at her back and shoulders, laughing the entire time. White dots twinkled in and out of her line of vision. Laying there, she prayed she would pass out before something worse happened to her. Curling into a ball, she lay there in agony as her legs, arms, and back were slashed repeatedly. Abruptly, the taunting laughter stopped, replaced by blood-curdling screams. She wondered if she was the one screaming. Incoherent and probably bleeding to death, she stayed completely still, afraid to even open her eyes. After a few minutes, the screaming stopped, the forest falling completely silent.

Through the haze, she swore she heard a man's voice talking, but the sound was faint. Then, something or someone rolled her over onto her back. Scared of what it might be, she forced her eyes back open. What she saw stunned her. Kade was staring down at her, his amazingly green eyes filled with worry. His mouth was moving, but she couldn't make out the words. She wasn't sure if she wanted to kiss him or smack him. After all, he was the reason she'd gone to that god-forsaken lake in the first place. Opening her mouth, she intended to yell at him, but all that came out was blood. Kade picked her up, tucking her tightly against his chest. Her wounds pressed against his body, causing her entire body to seize in agony. Closing her eyes again, she finally passed out.

Chapter 21

When Ava woke up, she was lying on a pallet made of dried leaves, inside the mouth of a vast cave. There was a blue fire burning in the corner, keeping the air nice and cool. How many times in the last week had she woken up not knowing what was going on? Way too F-ING many, she thought.

Kade was pacing back and forth just outside the cave, holding a huge hunting knife in one hand and an axe in the other. Sensing she was awake, he walked inside, laid down his weapons, then gently brushed the dirty hair away from her face. His green eyes were ablaze, lighting up the space with a warm glow.

"How are you feeling?" he asked.

Slowly sitting up, she expected to feel an onslaught of pain. When there was none, she patted all around her body, feeling nothing but smooth, unmarred skin.

Confused, Ava stared up at him. "Physically? I feel fine. Mentally? Not so much. How long was I out for?"

"Just a few hours," he said as he sat down next to her.

Amazed, she looked over her healed skin once again. "Where are all my wounds?"

Shrugging nonchalantly, he said, "I healed them. Luckily, I found you when I did. Five more minutes with those shadows and your injuries would have been too severe for even me to fix. Now that you're awake, we need to move deeper inside the cave. It's not safe being exposed out here!"

The way he said it stunned her. He was totally calm about it. In her world, people didn't just heal other people with their Jedi mind powers. The whole thing warranted a severe Q&A session. Come to think of it; she was sick of getting zero answers. For the past five days, nothing had made sense. It was time for him to hold up his end of the bargain.

Determined, she crossed her arms over her chest and glared at him. "I'm not going anywhere until you tell me what I want to know! In my dream, you promised it would all make sense. News flash, it still doesn't!

He smirked at her. The big jerk thought her ranting was funny. "Did you know your nose scrunches up when you're mad? It's the cutest thing! Now seriously, move it, or I'll move it for you!"

Cute!! Cute!! She was so mad she could spit! "I already said I'm not moving until you talk!"

He glanced over at her, this time with pure amusement in his eyes. "Fine! Have it your way!"

He moved so fast she couldn't track him. One minute, she was sitting on the floor, and the next, she was deep inside the cave, hanging upside down over his shoulder. The jerky movement caused her stomach to do a flip flop, and she almost threw up on him. Pounding on his back, she yelled, "Please put me down! I'm going to be sick!"

Kade complied, sliding her down his big body to stand on her feet. Being right-side-up didn't help anything, and she immediately dry-heaved. Kade pulled her hair out of the way, rubbing her back in small circles while she wretched for several minutes. Exhausted, she crumbled down on the cave floor and waited for him to start talking. He sat down across from her, creating another makeshift fire with the light from his hands. Then, he looked over at her and sighed.

"Over the past few days, you've experienced a lot of unexplainable things, but I'm still not sure you're ready for what I'm about to tell you."

Laughing nervously, she said, "Prepared? What are you even talking about!? Do you think I was prepared to be drowned, almost eaten by a flying sea monster, or sliced up by some weird shadowy things? Oh, and all that stuff happened in a place that I can only assume is Hell! I will never be prepared for anything you have to say. Do your worst!"

His shoulders slumped down in defeat, but he continued, "I didn't technically drown that day at the lake when I went missing. The same thing that happened to you happened to me. This place is called the in-between, and you may know it better as Purgatory."

"Purgatory? As in the place between Heaven and Hell?" she asked mockingly.

"Yes. But, the reality of this place takes a little more explaining. Purgatory is a place for souls who have not proven to be light or dark. If a soul is proven worthy of grace, it can be re-born in the Heavens. If not, some get to stay here. The rest, the darkest of them, get a one-way ticket downstairs. The souls here can be influenced or swayed to one side or the other, just like human souls on Earth. But you and I are different, separate from the influence."

Still feeling confused, Ava pressed him for more information. "You said you didn't technically drown. What does that mean? Are we alive?"

"Yes, Ava. We are both alive, and we came here with our mortal bodies. The fact that we're still tethered to them is why our souls can't be influenced."

She was relieved to know they were still alive, but her mind was reeling. What Kade was saying sounded true in a biblical sense, but she never believed in any of that stuff until today. Her parents weren't religious, and she'd chosen to be agnostic, refusing to buy into organized religion. She'd always been more of a seeing is believing type of person. But now, having seen this horrible place for herself, she wished she could go back to being ignorant. If she and Kade were stuck here alive, could they ever go back? Was that even possible?

Needing more clarification, she asked, "So, we're different because we're the only two people who are technically alive in this place?"

He glanced around nervously before answering. "That's partly why," he paused, "The other reason is, well, you're not a hundred percent human, and I, I'm not sure what I am anymore."

She swallowed hard. There was no way she'd heard him correctly. "Come again?"

As usual, he ignored her question and just kept on talking, "The lake acts as a portal between the human realm and this one. Some of the corrupted souls have gained enough power to leave this place and travel into our realm on Earth."

Ava wrapped her arms around herself for comfort. "Like the shadows that attacked me in the bathroom?"

"Yes, those souls were sent to harm you. Luckily, your father gave me the power to dream walk and appointed me as your guardian. We've been watching you for a long time. With your eighteenth birthday approaching, it was even more important to keep you safe until the time was right to bring you here. I was on my way to meet you at the portal when I was attacked."

At the mention of her father, she blanked out the rest. "My father! What are you talking about? My father knows about this place too?"

Kade looked over with sympathy in his eyes. "I hate to be the one to tell you this, but I have no choice at this point. You were adopted."

Rolling her eyes, she said, "I've known that all my life! What does that have to do with......"

The light bulb went off. "You're talking about my birth, Father?"

He nodded. She'd always been curious about her birth parents, and as the years passed, the urge to discover where she'd come from had grown exponentially. Even though her parents had always been honest with her, they'd never been very forthcoming with the details about the adoption itself. Then later, when she finally considered asking them about it, she felt instant guilt and chickened out. Kade held more knowledge about her life than she'd ever imagined possible.

He waved his hand in front of her face. "Hey, Ava! Are you still with me?"

All she could do was nod while he kept talking.

"I was on my way to meet you on the other side when the shadows ambushed me. By the time I cut through them all, you were already here, being attacked in the forest. I'm so sorry, Ava! I'll never forgive myself for not getting to you in time!"

He said it with such conviction that it made her heart skip a beat. She reached out and took his hand in hers.

"It's fine! You did the best you could, and thanks to you, I'm healed."

She held up her arms in response. "Look not a scratch now!"

"I know, but it should never have happened!" he said with shame in his eyes.

"What does my father have to do with any of this?"

Still looking away, he answered, "There's no way to sugarcoat this, so here goes. Your father is an angel. To be more accurate, a fallen angel."

Unable to contain herself, she laughed.

"You know, you almost had me buying into the whole Purgatory thing for a minute. But now, you're just talking nonsense!"

Frustrated, he let go of her hand and stood up.

"Nonsense? After everything you've seen the past few days, you still can't open your mind to the possibility? When was the last time you were sick? That would be a big never! Your angel DNA prevents you from getting any kind of human illnesses."

Standing, he sighed. "I know how farfetched this all sounds, but the sooner you come to grips with the truth, the better. Believe me; I know what you're going through. Barely four years ago, I was a normal high school freshman. Now, I'm stuck in Purgatory, assigned to guard the daughter of an angel!"

He was right, but it still didn't prove his claim. "I want to believe you, but for now, can you just tell me more about my father."

Calming down a bit, Kade leaned up against the cave wall. "His name is Samuel. I'm not sure if you're familiar with the war in Heaven, but an angel named Lucifer revolted against God during that time. Samuel remained neutral and refused to choose a side. Because of that, he was then cast out of Heaven along with Lucifer and the other fallen. But unlike them, Samuel didn't end up on Earth or in Hell. God created a special job for him. I guess a special punishment would be more apropos. Samuel must remain in Purgatory and watch over the lost souls trapped here. His ultimate job is to help them redeem themselves and find their way back into Heaven. The souls who can't be rehabilitated as you might call it, stay here, or eventually end up in Hell."

"Why did God give Samuel a "special" punishment?" she asked, perplexed.

"Because he loved him more than most. I'm not sure if you're aware of the different casts of angels?

She shook her head no. "My adoptive parents and I are agnostic."

Laughing, he said, "That's ironic, considering the truth. Well, there are several casts of angels that do different jobs. Samuel was a throne, one of the three highest casts. His job was to counsel and companion other angels and carry out divine judgments from God. Samuel disagreed with the divine judgment cast upon Lucifer. Therefore, his punishment is to counsel and judge all lost souls."

He reached out and squeezed her hand reassuringly. "We can take a break if you need one. I know this is a lot of information to process all at once."

"Honestly, my brain feels like mush, but I want to know everything. Keep going, please."

He kept a tight grip on her hand, finally sitting down across from her. "As I said before, the reason you and I are immune to the influence is because we don't belong here. We didn't die like the rest of the souls. This is my real body, and my soul is still inside. Same with you."

He stared down at their joined hands for a long time, then looked back up at her with a smile. It was the first time she'd really seen him smile, and it transformed his already handsome face into something breathtaking. His smile reminded her of the high school boy she'd seen in the yearbook rather than the hardened man sitting in front of her now.

Snapping back to reality, she pulled her hand away from his. Now wasn't the time to be crushing on a guy. "If Samuel is my father, was I born here?"

"No. You were born on Earth. Samuel isn't sure why, but God granted him a reprieve from this place. Every hundred years, he can leave Purgatory and spend exactly one year on Earth. The last time he was on this reprieve, he met your mother. He didn't think it was possible to conceive children with a mortal, but by some miracle, you were born."

Over the years, she'd often wondered why her birth parents had given her up and what kind of people they might be. In all the crazy scenarios she'd come up with, none of them started with an A and ended with an L. The whole thing was insane.

Kade was still talking, but she interrupted him, "Where's my birth mother now?"

His expression grew tense, but he stared directly into her eyes as he answered, "She died Ava, I'm sorry."

"How?" she asked, her voice barely a whisper.

"Your mother and father fell in love quickly, and you were born before his year on Earth was up. He never told your mother who he really was because he didn't think she would have believed him. Even if he had, it's against the rules for angels to reveal themselves to humans unless it's vital. He didn't want to put a burden on her and pull you both into his world if he didn't have to, so on his last day on Earth, he told your mother he had to leave on a business trip for a few days and never came back. Samuel doesn't have to use a portal like other souls because he isn't one. He can simply flash himself back and forth from Purgatory and Earth. It's sort of like teleportation."

He paused. "Are you sure you want to hear the rest? It's not pretty."

"Yes!" she answered, her voice another whisper.

"The flash leaves an energy trail between the worlds. Your father knew that, but at the time, he didn't have any reason to worry about it. He didn't know the shadows were gaining strength and able to escape Purgatory through the portal. After Samuel returned, the shadows followed his energy trail back to your mother's house. They killed her, Ava, just to hurt him."

She'd never met the woman, but the story was so sad, she couldn't hold back the tears.

"Samuel was stuck back in Purgatory and unaware of what was happening. Worse, even if he had known, he wouldn't have been able to save her. Luckily, they'd left you with a babysitter that day. Your mother didn't have any living family left, so after she died, the State put you up for adoption."

Pulling her into his lap, he wrapped his strong arms around her and held her as she cried. Gently stroking her hair, he asked, "Why don't you try and get some sleep, and we can talk more later?"

She stared up at him through blurry eyes. "I don't think I could sleep even if I wanted to."

Smiling down at her, he said, "I can help with that. Just close your eyes, and I'll do the rest. I don't think we should leave the cave until morning anyway."

She obeyed, instantly falling asleep.

Chapter 22

The next morning, Ava awoke still wrapped up in Kade's arms. After what felt like years of waking up scared and confused, it was comforting to remember exactly how she'd fallen asleep and with whom. Sadly, her peace of mind was short-lived. The moment she remembered where they were, all her anxiety and uncertainty came roaring back. Purgatory! They were in Purgatory. When she looked up, he was smiling down at her. Feeling uneasy about the situation, she sat up and quickly moved off his lap. She just didn't trust herself when he smiled at her like that.

"Sleep well?" he asked.

"Yes. Thank you for helping me relax with your weird mind mojo. I don't think I could have fallen asleep without it."

"You're welcome. And for what it's worth, I'm impressed by how well you're taking everything."

She ran her fingers through her hair in a feeble attempt to brush out the tangles. "I still feel like this is just another bad dream."

He stood up, dusting off his pants. "I wish it was."

"What now?" she asked.

"Now, we try and make it to Samuel's home as quickly as possible. I need to get you somewhere safe until I can figure out what to do next. Once we leave this cave, I need you to stay behind me the entire time.

If I ask you to do something, do it without question. Okay?"

Rolling her eyes, she said, "Yes, sir!"

Suddenly, Kade appeared right in front of her. Startled, she jumped backward, but he grabbed onto her shoulders and forced her to stay in place. Glaring down at her, he said, "This isn't a game, Ava! You've already seen some of the horrors in this place, but you have no idea what else is out there. I'm asking you to listen to me for your own protection. Please take this seriously!"

She swallowed hard, nodding.

When they exited the cave, he told her it was still morning, but she couldn't tell the difference since the sky looked the same as it had the night before. The forest sat directly in front of them, but instead of going in, he walked around to the opposite side of the cave, where a dirt path wound up the side of the mountain. She was thankful they didn't have to travel back through the forest. Just thinking about what the shadows had done to her made her entire body shudder.

Kade walked in front of her, holding her hand in one of his hands, while he held the gigantic hunting knife in the other. The higher they climbed up the mountain, the steeper and more treacherous the path became. She was clumsy on a good day, and the uneven terrain was almost impossible to navigate. Stumbling and tripping all over herself, she tried to keep up with him as best she could. His quick flashing power came in quite handy when she needed someone to catch her. Thankfully, he was right there, every time, steadying her before she ate dirt.

For a long time, all she could see was the black rock as they continued up the side of the mountain.

After what felt like hours, they finally rounded a sharp corner and stepped out onto an open ledge. From their high vantage point, the burning mountains seemed to stretch on forever. Ava could even see the outline of the lake that had brought her to this hellish place. From this height, it looked like a tiny blip in the middle of a world on fire. Just ahead of them was another path, continuing higher up the mountain. Kade pulled her along, heading straight for it. Fire and smoke billowed out of the rocks on both sides. Terrified, she stopped walking.

Urging her forward, he said, "I know it looks bad, but I've got a few more tricks up my sleeve."

Nervous, she still hesitated. "How are we going to walk any further without getting burned?"

"Do you trust me?" he asked.

Did she? She asked herself. If she was being honest, she had no real reason not to trust him. He had already saved her life once. If he had nefarious intentions, then why save her, just to put her in danger now.

"Yes, Kade. I do," she answered truthfully.

"Good! We're going to be fine. Close your eyes if you need to."

As they approached the path, the flames were so close that her skin began to sting. She was about to question Kade's judgment when the air around them began to shimmer with a bright iridescent glow. The glow covered them from head to toe, finally disappearing at their feet. She looked at Kade, dumbfounded. Again!

"It's like a second skin. It protects me and anything I'm touching. Unfortunately, it doesn't protect me from anything but fire, so stay close and don't let go of my hand."

Ava huddled up as close to his back as possible as they walked on under the onslaught of flames. She was still terrified the "skin" might fail at any moment, and they would both burn to death. For the time being, it held, shielding them from the burning inferno. Even though the flames couldn't reach them, the smoke was still thick, and she had no idea how he could see two feet in front of them. Slowly, the flames began to dissipate, and the landscape evened out to form another clearing. This one was free of fire, but what she saw instead stunned her. A half-mile ahead of them sat a huge castle. Complete with tall winding turrets and soaring gray stone walls that were dilapidated and crumbling. Just like everything else in this place, it looked dead and desolate.

"Whoa! Is that where Samuel lives?"

He laughed, "Yes. Home sweet home!"

She was struck with a wave of sadness. She couldn't believe Kade had been stuck here for years, living in a broken-down castle, like some prince in a dark, twisted fairy tale. He'd been so much younger than she was now when he'd first arrived in this horrible place. They were still a few hundred feet from the castle when it began to drizzle. The ground sizzled everywhere the raindrops landed. She glanced up at Kade, whose expression was filled with terror.

"RUN!" he yelled, pulling her along with him. A raindrop landed on her left arm as they ran, causing her skin to bubble and blister. It felt like getting hit with hot grease. If it started raining any harder, they were going to be in some serious shit.

"Kade...."

"Don't talk, just keep running!" he pleaded.

Ava got pegged by a few more drops before they finally made it inside the front gate of the castle. Her face, arm, and back all felt like they were on fire. Trying to be strong, she bit her lower lip to avoid crying out in pain. After they made it safely inside, he led her down a long hallway, finally stopping in front of a large wooden door. He waved his hand in front of it, and the thing swung open wide. Immediately, she recognized the room from one of her dreams. It looked exactly the same. It was in this very room that she'd witnessed him use the light from his hands for the first time. He walked her over to one of the high back chairs facing the fireplace and motioned for her to sit.

Then, he kneeled in front of her, running his hands up and down the sides of her body. Against her will, her body shivered in response to his touch. Embarrassed, she tried to focus on the pain instead of how good his hands felt on her skin.

Finally, he settled his hands on top of her shoulders. "Try to relax, and I'm going to fix the burns now."

Kade began mumbling in a language she didn't understand. It was beautiful and melodic. Instantly, she felt little pinches all over her body, and then the pain faded.

Captivated, she looked around the room. "Thank you! Again! Talk about Deja vu. How exactly did you bring me here while I was sleeping?"

"I didn't," he said as he walked over to the other chair and slumped down into it. He had to be exhausted. He'd been fighting before he'd even found her.

"One of the powers Samuel gave me lets me visit you in your sleep. It lets me connect my soul with yours. When we're connected, you see what I see or where I am. We call it dream walking."

That made sense. "But how did I see you at school? I wasn't sleeping then, and I literally bumped right into you."

Kade smirked. "I wasn't really there. Honestly, I can't even begin to understand the magnitude of Samuel's powers or how he pulled off that one. For reasons unbeknownst to me, Samuel felt extra worried about you that day and didn't want to wait for you to fall asleep. Instead, he used some major power to teleport my soul to you at school, which took a lot out of him. You saw me but bumped into another student."

Laughing, she said, "How embarrassing. I really thought you were an ass for not apologizing. It turns out; I'm the ass."

Another thought popped into her head. "What about the other dreams?"

Shrugging, he asked, "What do you mean?"

"I had a dream about the portal before it happened, and when I woke up, I had bruises on my sides. How is that possible?"

He contemplated for a moment before answering her, "The shadows must have used your dreams as another kind of portal and somehow pulled your soul to the lake. Mirrors, water, even dreams can all act as portals if someone knows how to access them. Luckily, you woke up, and your soul snapped back into your body."

"But that doesn't explain the bruises or why everything smelled like sulfur?"

"Maybe because you are half-angel, your mind is powerful enough to manifest things like smells and the bruises."

Frowning, she said, "You think I did all that?"

"Don't know for sure, but that's my theory. You do realize you have powers, right?

"Really? I mean, I shot some weird white light out of my hands twice. But, both times, I didn't mean for it to happen. The first time, I tried to recreate it, but nothing happened."

The fireplace was right in front of them, and she decided there was no time like the present to try it again. Raising both of her hands, she flapped them around in the direction of the fireplace, but nothing happened.

Laughing, Kade said, "What in the world are you doing?"

"Trying to use my powers. DUH! Instead of laughing at me, why don't you show me how you do it?"

He stood up, moving closer to the fireplace. "I don't know how to explain it. My powers were given to me, whereas yours are natural. When Samuel gave me some of his power, it was in a brief ceremony. He mixed some of our blood, mouthed an incantation, and then poof, I was instantly able to do all kinds of things with just a thought."

Aggravated, Ava crossed her arms over her chest and huffed. "Lucky, you! Why don't you go ahead and do it then? It's getting really hot in here."

Sighing, he said, "You shouldn't give up so easily. Have a little faith in yourself!"

Annoyed, she railed at him, "That's the problem, Kade; I've never had any faith. After everything that's happened to me over the past few days, I feel like my entire life is a sham. Last week I was agnostic. This week, I'm a half-angel with magical powers! Excuse me if I'm off my A-game!"

He walked over, pulling her out of the chair.

"What are you doing?" she asked in a shaky voice.

"It's okay if you don't have faith yet. For now, just believe in yourself and try. Let's do it together."

He stepped behind her, slowly running his hands down her arms. When he reached her hands, he lifted them in the air so they were facing the fireplace.

"Alright, now relax and close your eyes," he commanded.

Ava wasn't sure if she could relax with him touching her like he was, but she closed her eyes anyway.

"Now, let everything go. Remember you're safe here with me. Know that I won't let anything bad happen to you."

His mouth was so close that she could feel his warm breath fanning out over her skin. Gently pressing herself back into him, she tried to relax. He was so much bigger than she was, but she liked the way they fit together.

"Good," he whispered, "Last time this happened, what were you feeling?'

"The first time, anger. The second time, terror."

He rubbed his thumbs over her palms. "Sounds to me like your emotions are the trigger for your powers. What emotion are you feeling the most right now?"

Ava swallowed hard. The pleasure was at the top of the list, with all the touching going on, but she didn't want to admit that to him. Instead, she said, "Gratitude, for everything you've done for me." It wasn't a total lie.

He kissed her softly on the cheek. "Again, you're welcome. Now, try to focus on that feeling and pour all the energy you have into your hands."

"I don't know how," she whispered.

"Imagine the gratitude you feel as a tangible thing. Picture it as a white light flowing through you, building up in the center of your body. Once you can see it, push it down through your arms and into your hands."

She visualized the light and instantly felt a warm sensation journey down her arms. It was exciting! "Kade! I feel something!"

"Good. Keep your eyes closed and picture all that energy flowing out from your hands and into the fireplace. You can do it, Ava; I'm right here with you."

At first, her hands felt like they were filling up with something heavy; they even burned a little, but not in a painful way. She imagined the fireplace erupting with light, and the pressure in her hands immediately disappeared. Opening her eyes, she was shocked to find the fireplace ablaze with white light.

"Amazing!" Was the only word Ava could muster as she stared into the flames.

"Yes, you are!" he said, lightly kissing the back of her neck.

The sensation sent her mind and body racing. Kade spun her around before she had time to react and brought his hand up under her chin. He tilted her face up to his, staring down at her with hunger in his eyes. Green eyes that were now glowing as bright as the fire.

"You're so beautiful," he whispered, just as he pressed his lips against hers.

Chapter 23

The kiss was exciting and unexpected! She'd been attracted to him since the first time she'd seen him but never thought it a million years that he might feel the same way. His lips fit perfectly against hers. When he finally pulled away, it was all too soon, leaving her feeling cold and empty.

After taking a deep breath, he said, "I've been wanting to do that for a long time."

Blushing, she turned her face away from his to hide her reaction.

Sensing her unease, he reached out and gently turned her face back toward his. "Did I do something wrong?"

"No, I just.... I don't know what to say. That was my first kiss!"

He smirked. "Really? How is that possible? I mean, the boys at school must flock all over you."

For some reason, she felt compelled to explain her non-existent love life to him. "You've got it all wrong. Aside from one guy at my old school, members of the opposite sex tend to avoid me like the plague."

Cocking a brow at her, he said, "Then clearly everyone you've met is either blind or stupid because you're the most beautiful girl I've ever seen."

No one had ever said that to her before. "My eyes are kind of weird. Haven't you noticed?"

Sighing, he pulled her closer to him. "Your eyes are the best part about your face. When I look in them, it's like I can see to your soul."

Her pulse spiked again as he slowly stroked his hand down the side of her face. "As much as I'd like to stay here with you, we have to find Samuel."

Samuel should have about eighty-one more years before his next reprieve based on what Kade had previously explained to her. Confused once again, she asked, "What do you mean, find him? Isn't he here?"

He looked worried. "Yes and No. I mean, he's somewhere in Purgatory since he can't physically leave, but I haven't been able to locate him. He was kidnapped a few days ago, and I don't know where he is."

"Kidnapped?" she still didn't understand. "How can an angel, who is supposed to be the ruler of this place, get kidnapped?"

Kade shook his head. "I don't know the answer! But I do know that he would never just up and disappear when we were in the middle of watching over you! Remember I told you about the shadows I was fighting when you came through the portal? Well, they have been gaining power for years, and Samuel has been trying to stop them ever since your mother was killed. Most of the angels that were cast out of heaven remain on Earth, but sometimes an angel's soul ends up in Purgatory. It's rare for an angel to be killed, but it is possible. A few millennia ago, an angel named Amon was sent here. He had committed such heinous acts on Earth that he wasn't a candidate for any kind of rehabilitation. So instead, Samuel bound him in the worst part of Purgatory."

"You mean there are worse places than the ones I've already seen?" she asked, cringing at the thought.

"Yes, Ava, much worse. There are pits where souls burn with never-ending flames and caverns filled with terrifying monsters, much worse than the one you saw in the lake. Samuel knew that Amon was the only one capable of giving the shadows a power boost and had been searching for him for years. Around the same time your mother was murdered, Amon somehow escaped his confinement."

She didn't understand how any of this could have happened. "How did Amon get out? Is he more powerful than my father?"

"At this point, I honestly don't know. Samuel believed Amon was absorbing the evil souls in Purgatory, attempting to gain more power. Once Amon absorbs a soul, he can use it at his command, giving and taking power from it. Samuel believes that Amon is the one responsible for the missing kids at Devil's Head Lake. An innocent soul, one not meant to end up in Purgatory, holds immense power. Much more than any of the corrupted souls here. When I came through the portal, I was lucky Samuel found me before Amon did. In all the time I've been here, I've never seen any of the other people. You and I both know what that means. Either Amon took them, or they died by other means. I also think Amon is the one who took Samuel, but I don't know how."

Ava felt the need to comfort him and intertwined her fingers with his. As she did, some of the stress evaporated from his face. "We've come this far, and we will find him! I don't have faith in a religious sense, but I do have faith in you!"

He smiled briefly, heading towards the door.

"Over time, Samuel amassed a small army of good souls that helped him keep the order. Sadly, most of them have also gone missing. The few that remain are helping me look for him and should report back tomorrow. In the meantime, it's just you and me. I think we should start where Amon was being held and backtrack from there. Samuels army has already checked out the area, but I want to see it for myself. Its location is close to the lake portal, and Amon would have needed a place nearby to send the shadows back and forth. She didn't want to go anywhere near the lake, but what other choice did she have? It's not like she could just sit and wait for Kade to come back, and it would be game over if Amon or some other monster came for her while he was gone.

Reluctantly, she replied, "Alright, let's get this over with."

Gripping her hand tightly, he said, "Same rules as before. I say jump; you say how high!"

They walked out of the castle and down the side of the burning mountain. This time, Ava wasn't as worried since she knew his shield would keep them safe. But as they walked on, she wondered more about his presence here, specifically, why Samuel hadn't just sent him back home when he'd initially found him.

Tapping him on the shoulder, she pressed for more answers. "I know how you got here, but what happened afterward? At first, you didn't have any powers, so how did you survive until Samuel found you?"

He slowed his pace as he answered, "Honestly, I just got lucky and made it out of the lake before any of the sea creatures found me. I'm still not sure where the monsters here originated. I asked Samuel about it a few times, but he always seemed uncomfortable talking about the origins of this place. So, after a while, I stopped asking. To this day, I still don't know if this place already existed or if God created it from scratch. I don't know if the monsters were already here or if someone created them."

She felt disgusted. "Why would someone create such evil monsters? What would be the purpose? If some of the souls here have a chance at redemption, why would Samuel want to subject them to things like that?"

He stopped walking and turned around to face her. "I wish I had more answers for you, but on this topic, I don't. What I do know, to the core of my being, is that

Samuel is good. I doubt he put them here, but If he did, he had his reasons!"

Ava didn't know Samuel from Adam, she thought. But she did know Kade. If he trusted Samuel, then she would try to trust him as well.

"After I made it to the forest, I was encased in the same mist you saw, but at the time, it was much higher and reached up to the tree branches. The level of it changes based on the time of day. Fun fact, the mist seeps into your skin, slowly choking you from the inside out. The day you came through, it was low enough not to affect you, but it can take a person over easily as it rises. I only made it about an hour before passing out, and when I woke up, I was in Samuel's castle. For weeks, I just paced around my room, refusing to believe all the things he was telling me. Eventually, though, I had to accept it. Just as you have."

In that moment, Ava felt such a deep connection with him. They were literally the only two people in the world who could compare notes on what it was like to be trapped in Purgatory. She was thankful Samuel had rescued him, but it still didn't seem right.

"Why didn't he just send you back?"

He shrugged. "He tried. But for some reason, it didn't work. I can travel back and forth through the portal, but my time and range on the human side is limited. I can only stay for about an hour or travel about a mile out in each direction before I'm pulled back in. After Samuel failed to relocate me permanently, he finally gave in to the notion that I must have ended up here for a reason. Like maybe God was blocking his powers to keep me here. I didn't think there was much merit to any of that until he sent me to you."

She was getting sick of blushing, but her face heated uncontrollably. "What do you mean?"

He looked deep into her eyes as he spoke, "The first time I saw you, I felt something inside me shift. I can't explain it, but I just knew we were meant to be together. I know you haven't known me for very long, but I've been watching you for months."

She felt it, too, some uncontrollable pull towards him that she'd never felt before. Even though she wanted to tell him how she felt, the words got stuck in her throat.

In response to her non-response, he gently stroked her cheek before turning back around. To his credit, he didn't even seem offended.

Ava inwardly cursed at herself. A fantastic guy just told her he thought they were meant to be together, and she couldn't even muster up the strength to tell him she liked him back. Once they made it to the bottom of the mountain, he continued telling his story.

"When Amon broke free, Samuel knew it was only a matter of time before he came for him, so he's been training me in all aspects of combat since I first arrived. My powers came easily, but my training did not. It was a long, grueling process, but Samuel made sure I'd be able to protect myself and you, if necessary. He told me that if anything ever happened to him, I was to bring you here immediately. So, after he went missing, I sent you the dream, asking you to meet me at the lake."

Everything he was saying made sense, except her part in it. "Why did you need to get me? I understand him wanting you to watch over me after what happened to my mother, but why bring me here? This place isn't safe."

After they were clear of all the flames, he motioned for her to sit down in the clearing.

"You're the first angel human hybrid that's ever existed. We already know you have some powers, but the scope of them is unknown. If Amon has amassed enough power to take down Samuel, then you might be the only hope we have to save him."

Chapter 24

"Come again?" Ava asked sarcastically. Seriously though, who was Kade kidding? She barely had control over the one power she knew she possessed. Now, he expected her to go toe to toe with a full-blown angel. Her head spun as the nightmare of their situation kept getting worse.

Kade lightly rubbed her back. "Take some nice deep breaths and try to calm down."

Laughing nervously, she said, "Yeah, right! How am I supposed to calm down! Three days ago, I was a normal seventeen-year-old, who's only problem was having less than stellar parents and zero boyfriend prospects. Today, I find out I have powers and might have to save my angel of a father from some other evil angel. Yeah, totally fine here, really, just fine!"

Her nervous laughing turned into full-blown hysterics. It was inappropriate, but it sounded so ridiculous that all she could do was crack up when she said it all aloud. After everything she'd been through, it was a miracle she hadn't cracked before now.

Pulling her in for a tight hug, he said, "Ava, you can do this! I beat the odds and am standing here for a reason. That reason is you! You have to believe that you have a bigger purpose, regardless of how impossible it might sound."

Melting into his arms, she said, "There you go with that faith talk again. Like I told you before, it's hard for me to believe in anything that I can't see!"

He pulled her hands up to his chest and pressed them tightly against it. "Then just keep believing in me. I'm right here in front of you. You can see me. Feel me!"

Ava wasn't sure if believing in him alone would be enough to overcome what was standing in front of them. He was so sure they had a higher purpose, but what if that was all bull shit. Looking up into his unbelievably green eyes, she wanted to tell him everything would be okay, but that would be a lie. The truth was, she had no idea what they were up against or if she could deliver on his expectations. The only thing she knew for sure was that she had the courage to try with him by her side, and that was better than giving up. They were practically in Hell already; what was the worst that could happen? If there really was a Heaven, maybe dying would be a better solution than being stuck here. Even if they somehow defeated Amon, Samuel still didn't have the power to send Kade back, which meant he might not be able to send her back either.

Wrapping his arms around her waist, he pulled her closer to him. He kissed her gently, pushing the troubling thoughts out of her mind. The kiss started soft but quickly turned feverish. Two seconds later, a horrible screeching noise broke them apart.

Kade jumped up, immediately pushing her behind him. "Grab onto my belt loop and don't let go!"

That's when she saw them. Dozens of black shadows were slinking out of the cracks in the mountain. As they broke free, the depraved laughter began. It was the same sound she'd heard in the woods while being brutally attacked. Stepping forward, he pulled his hunting knife out of its sheath. One shadow after another tried to attack him, but he moved at hyper speed, flashing left and right with her in tow. By holding onto his belt, she flashed whenever he did. It felt like being on a roller coaster. It was an exhilarating but blurry experience. Every time Kade stopped, it was only for a brief second to allow him enough time to swing out his knife. Whenever he hit a shadow, it exploded into a pile of shiny black rocks. The rocks were piling up all around them. Kade flashed again, but this time one of the shadows tracked him, and when he stopped, it appeared right in front of him. Unable to dodge it, he took a hard blow to the chest that sent them flying backward. She landed on the ground, with him right on top of her. It hurt badly! If Kade was feeling the pain, too, he didn't show it. Instead, he launched himself right back up and attacked the shadow closest to them.

This time when he flashed away, she forgot to hold onto him. Realizing the error, she backed herself up against a rock, as far out of the way as possible. Then, she watched in awe as he dogged and danced all around the shadows. He was beautiful and lethal. All his movements were so calculated and precise from his years of training. She was so mesmerized by him that she didn't notice the shadow sneaking up beside her. It grabbed her roughly by the throat, picking her up off the ground. She tried to yell to Kade, but its hand was strangling her so hard it cut off her windpipe. Adrenaline pumping, she tried to claw at the hand around her neck but felt nothing. It was just like the shadowy one from the lake and held no solid form. The pressure around her neck increased just as she heard Kade cry out in pain.

Hearing his pained voice snapped her out of her own panic long enough for her to try and focus on using her powers. Just as she began to picture the white light, Kade's knife struck through the middle of the shadow holding her. Upon contact, the shadow exploded all around them in a cascade of shining rock. Falling, Kade caught her in his arms just before she hit the ground. Gently, he laid her down, placing his hands around her neck, and she felt the familiar heat spread throughout her body as he healed her again. Sitting up, she frantically looked him over for wounds.

On his right side, just above his hip, she found a large bloody gash. "Oh my god! You're bleeding everywhere!"

He pressed his hand against the wound, and in response, more blood gushed out. Through gritted teeth, he said, "It's fine! Just a surface wound."

Kade tried to stand up but swayed on his feet. Ava helped him sit back down, looking around nervously the entire time. He must have taken care of all the shadows because there were none left in sight.

Worried, she said, "You're so not okay! There's blood everywhere, and you can barely stand!"

He didn't argue with her. Instead, he just leaned up against the rock, breathing heavily. "I've had worse. Just need a few minutes to rest, and then we can keep going."

She seriously doubted that. Kade's wound was massive, and the bleeding wasn't slowing down. "I'm guessing you don't have the power to heal yourself?"

His non-response was all the answer she needed. "Yeah. That's what I thought. We're not going to get anywhere if you bleed out against that rock. You think I possess all these powers, right? Well, it's time to see what I can do. If I can't help you, then this is all over before it even starts. I have no idea how to find Amon or Samuel without you!"

Gripping his side harder, he sighed. "I don't know if you have the power to heal, and Samuel has no idea what powers you may or may not have inherited."

Leaning over his wound, she placed both of her hands over the area that was gushing blood. Inside, she was freaking out, but she didn't want him to know it, so as calmly as possible, she asked, "Any advice on how to make this work?"

He winced. "Try the same thing as before. Picture the light inside of you, and then visualize what you want. This time, instead of creating fire, focus on closing my wound."

Closing her eyes, she did what he asked. At first, nothing happened. She didn't understand why it wasn't working as it had back in the castle. Tears pooled in her eyes. She couldn't let him down. Not after everything he'd done for her. Not after all the horrible things that he'd endured in this place. Just the thought of it all filled her with rage. He should never have ended up here, having his life and innocence stripped away—year by year.

She was about to give up when she heard him groan in pain. Opening her eyes to check on him, she was amazed by what she saw. His wound was closed entirely.

"You did it!" he beamed.

She was still stunned. "I started thinking about all the things you've been through because of this awful place, and it made me furious!"

Standing on solid legs, he pulled her up with him. Then, he used his shirt to wipe all the blood off her hands. "You already knew your emotions play into your powers. Anger is a huge trigger; remember that for next time."

She vowed to remember it, take a picture of it, write it down. Whatever it took to protect them both. As they walked away, she turned back to look at the large pool of blood on the ground, and for the first time, she felt thankful to be more than just human.

Chapter 25

They kept moving towards the place where Amon had once been held. Ava expected them to pass back through the forest, ending up beachside, but instead, Kade informed her they were taking a shortcut. This time, they walked past the cave entrance toward a vast marshland filled with blood-red water and various kinds of decaying debris. Swallowing hard, she wondered what kind of horrible monsters might be lurking under the surface.

As they neared the water, she covered her mouth and nose with both of her hands, trying not to gag. "Oh god! The smell."

The rancid smell of sulfur wafting from the water was unbearable. Kade took out his knife, cut two small pieces of clean cloth off the bottom of his shirt, and handed one to her. He put his piece of cloth over his nose and mouth, motioning for her to do the same. "It will help a little."

She doubted that but tried anyway. Kade continued towards the right side of the marsh, where a tiny patch of mud lay between the mountain and water.

"I think we're going to have to go all the way around. I don't see any other way for us to cross, short of getting in," he said.

Ava didn't like the thought of being so close to the water but had no other choice. Walking around was a thousand times better than having to get in it physically.

"Haven't you been this way before?" she asked.

He shook his head. "No. One of Samuel's soldiers told me about this shortcut after they went looking for him the first time."

Great, she thought, just great. The marsh was so vast; she couldn't even see the other side from where they were standing. As they got closer to the mud path, she noticed the red water bubbling up in several spots. When the disgusting bubbles popped at the surface, they released a thick white mist into the air. Wondering if that was where the sulfur smell was coming from, she tried to avoid breathing anywhere near the mist pockets. After walking for a long while, her tennis shoes began sinking into the thick, gross mud. It wasn't pleasant, but at least nothing had attacked them. Yet! She was trying her best to keep quiet in case dangerous creatures were hiding in the marsh, but her head was still swimming with questions.

"Kade?" she whispered, "If and when we find Amon, what exactly is the plan?"

He slowed a little. "Honestly, I'm hoping we can find Samuel without having to deal with Amon at all. I don't want to risk either of our lives if I don't have to. We need Samuel to get rid of Amon, so he's priority number one."

She agreed. She didn't want to try to fight Amon with powers she didn't fully understand. "Why did Amon kidnap him anyway? What exactly does he want?"

"Amon thinks he can use Samuel's powers to get back into Heaven."

"And that's a bad thing? Ava asked, "I mean, I know he's evil, but wouldn't sending him back to Heaven fix our problem? I mean, if he went back, wouldn't God be forced to deal with him instead of Samuel?"

Huffing, he said, "It's not that simple. When God charged Samuel with running Purgatory, he made it impossible for any souls to go to Heaven or Hell without Samuel's approval. If a soul were to escape Purgatory somehow and find its way back into Heaven without Samuel's stamp of approval, then it would corrupt the whole system. Amon isn't a soul exactly, but the rules still apply to him because he ended up in Purgatory. Ava, if

Amon gets back into Heaven, it would jump-start the apocalypse. Heaven, Hell, and Purgatory would all bleed together into the human world. Angels and demons would be forced to war against each other on Earth, destroying everything in their path."

She had gotten used to hearing crazy news over the past few days, but this one took the cake. Not only were they in immediate danger, but the entire world was at risk. If they didn't find Samuel soon, her parents, friends, and everyone she'd ever known could potentially die. The weight of it all rocked her to the core of her being.

"I'll do whatever I can to save him!" she exclaimed and meant it even if it meant giving up her own life. Who was she in relation to the whole world? No one, she thought. They had to find Samuel, and they had to do it fast. They kept a decent pace, walking through the muck for what felt like hours. Every time the marsh bubbled or something splashed, she jumped in response. Eventually, they came to a spot where the path dead-ended into the woods. He took her by the hand as they walked inside.

"Are these the same woods we were in before?" she asked. They seemed similar but felt very different.

Shaking his head, he said, "No, we're on the other side of the mountain now."

The trees here weren't oozing blood, but they were emitting a strange high-pitched humming sound. When she walked too close to one, the hair on her arm stood up. Kade grabbed her roughly, quickly pulling her back.

"Don't touch anything! The trees on this side carry an electrical charge. I've seen the shadows bump up against them, and when they do, they immediately turn to dust. I don't have a shield for this kind of stuff, so be careful. The holding area is only about a mile up ahead. Please try to stay alive until we reach it."

Ava rolled her eyes but followed closely behind him, stepping wherever he stepped. When they finally reached the holding area, there was nothing there. It was strange. One minute, they were walking through the forest, and the next, they were surrounded by nothing but darkness. Taking a step backward, the forest reappeared all around her. Confused and fascinated, she stepped forward again, instantly surrounded by darkness.

"It's a cloaking spell," he explained. "Samuel used it to hide Amon so that the other souls couldn't find him. Even if they had stumbled upon this place while Amon was still locked inside, all they would have seen was the darkness. A pretty cool trick if you ask me."

While he searched the area, looking for clues as to how Amon had escaped, she kept walking in and out of the cloaking area. It was just so strange to be in the forest one second and then literally nowhere the next. The third time she walked in, a large bright star appeared a few feet away from her. It shimmered like a diamond, and she felt compelled to touch it. In the back of her mind, she thought she heard Kade yelling, but a loud swishing sound drowned him out. For a moment, she felt like she was being sucked into a wind tunnel, and then abruptly, everything stopped.

Looking around, she found herself standing alone in the middle of a burnt field. Seconds later, Kade came barreling out of nowhere right behind her, tripping over his own feet and face planting in the dirt. She couldn't hold back the laugh watching him eat it.

"Didn't you hear me yelling?" he asked.

Nodding, she said, "I thought I heard something, but it was too late to do anything about it."

"Good thing we ended up here and not somewhere worse. Samuel told me never to touch anything inside the containment area. He added a second spell as a fail-safe. I tried to grab you, but you disappeared before I could."

She pointed a finger in his face. "You didn't think it was pertinent to mention that BEFORE I went inside?"

Brushing himself off, he rolled his eyes. "It slipped my mind, and honestly, I didn't think you'd go all handsy. Next time, no touching!

We're lucky it spit me out in the same place as you. Come to think of it; it's weird that it did. I wouldn't think Samuel would want the shadows ending up in the same place together after looking for Amon. It would be more advantageous to send them all to different places."

She felt embarrassed. They were probably way off track now, just because she couldn't keep her hands to herself. "Where are we exactly?"

Peering around, Kade surveyed the area. "I have no idea!"

That wasn't reassuring, she thought. There was literally nothing around them but the burnt ground. Kade walked back over to the area where he'd popped out of thin air. "I'm going to try and use my powers to re-open whatever portal sent us here. Give me your hand. Maybe with our combined powers, we can make something happen."

She clasped her hands with his as he began chanting in that strange, beautiful language again. As she watched, a soft white light began pulsing between their joined fingers. After a few moments, he sighed in frustration and let go.

"Whatever magic Samuel used to send us here is way too powerful for us to reverse. Let's just start walking while I think for a minute."

She had no idea which way to go. "Um... Kade? Which direction do you want to walk in? I hate to bring this up, but there's nothing anywhere around us."

He seemed aggravated by her comment and began pacing. As he walked, she noticed what looked like a slight shimmer in the air beside him. She let him walk back and forth a few more times before mentioning it. But something was there. When he walked by a particular area to his left, the air trailed behind him for a moment, quickly fading back to normal.

"Kade stop walking!" she yelled.

Frustrated, he threw his hands up in the air. "Just let me think for a minute, will you!"

"No, I won't. Now stop being stubborn and look!!"

Resigned, he stopped and let her walk past him. As she did, she swished her hands around in the air. "Do you see the way the air is blurring like that?"

Kade walked forward to where she'd just been standing and stuck his arm straight out. His entire forearm disappeared into nothing.

"Nice trick!" he laughed.

She didn't understand. "What exactly are you laughing about?"

"It's another cloak. There's something on the other side; we just can't see it. Just like you can't see the holding area unless you know where it is or accidentally walk inside it."

Abruptly, he turned around and walked towards her. Reaching out, he grabbed her by the back of the neck and kissed her so intensely; she was breathless by the time he stopped.

"I don't know what's behind that wall, but you know I'll do everything in my power to protect you. If something happens to me, you need to find Samuel. You know what's at stake. If I'm gone, I want you to find Samuel's army. They're meeting back at the castle soon and will help you. If you must hide, hide until it's safe, but don't ever give up. Promise me!"

Just the thought of something happening to him made her want to vomit, but he was right. No matter what, she had to find Samuel and stop Amon from getting what he wanted.

"I promise!" she said, a tear rolling down her cheek. He took her hand in his, and together, they walked through the invisible wall.

Chapter 26

One minute, they were standing in the middle of the burnt wasteland, and the next, they were standing at the base of a mountain. One that wasn't on fire. A crumbling stone staircase wound up the center of it, ending high up on a jagged cliff. Sitting on top of the cliff was what appeared to be a small building, made of the same stone as Samuel's castle. Ava glanced around wearily. They were standing on what looked to be a floating island, with nowhere to go but up. She went for the stairs, but Kade stopped her.

"I don't think we should just walk right up. If Samuel is really in there, we need the element of surprise."

Dumfounded, she looked around again. A black void surrounded the island, and there was nothing but dark velvety night around it. Unless he wanted to jump off the side and see what happened, there was nowhere else to go.

"Kade, if Amon's in there," she said, pointing up towards the building, "Don't you think he already knows we're here? I mean, if it were me, I'd want to know when someone broke through the barrier to this place. I bet we already tripped some kind of mystical alarm system."

He took her hand in his. "You're probably right, but I still don't want to march up those steps blindly. Let's at least walk around the base of the mountain to see if there's another way in first."

She let him drag her past the stairs while he surveyed the area. The sides of the mountains were all sleek stone and had no footing for climbing. Unless Kade secretly had the power to fly, they'd be stair mastering it.

Suddenly, he stopped walking. "I don't like this. Something feels weird......" His words were cut off mid-sentence.

At the same time, her skin felt like it was being covered in pins and needles. "Kade! What's happening?"

He didn't answer her or move, and when she tried calling out to him again, her tongue wouldn't work. They were both frozen in place. She'd been right all along. Amon already knew they were here. All hope of saving Samuel vanished as she stared into Kade's terrified eyes. Then came the maniacal laughter, as shadow after shadow crawled down the side of the mountain, right behind Kade. They covered him like a swarm of locusts, wrapping him up until his body disappeared entirely under their inky black mass. Screaming inside her head, she watched in horror as they dragged him up the mountain.

The landscape blurred into darkness and then changed completely. In the blink of an eye, she was no longer standing on the floating island. Now, she was standing inside a cage, chained to the floor by her hands and feet. The silver chains that bound her gave her enough room to stand but not much else. When she turned around, she noticed another person in the cage with her. Frightened, she tried to take a step back, only to be pulled down to the ground by the chains. The man sitting in the cage with her was dirty and covered in dried blood. Aside from the grime, what startled her the most about him, were the familiar jet-black eyes staring back at her.

"Samuel?" she asked tentatively.

He nodded. Ava wasn't sure what she had expected, but this wasn't it. She thought he'd at least have wings. Sitting there in the corner, chained to the floor with her, he seemed like any other middle-aged man. He had porcelain white skin, with short jet-black hair that matched his jet-black eyes. Age-wise, he looked to be in his mid-thirties. She couldn't tell exactly how tall he was since he was sitting, but his legs were very long and covered in lean muscle. Aside from the eyes, she looked nothing like him.

"That's because you look just like your mother," he said, his voice velvety and beautiful.

She hadn't spoken aloud. "Did you just read my mind?"

Shrugging casually, he said, "The skill would be more useful if I could read the minds of souls and not just humans, but Que Sera. I didn't mean to invade your privacy, but it takes effort I don't have right now to block it out. I don't think anyone's coming back for a while so that we can speak freely."

Staring at him blankly, she tried not to think about anything. The cage was surrounded by walls, except for the front, which faced a narrow hallway, but the length of the chains prevented her from looking out.

"A bunch of shadows just dragged Kade away, and I ended up here. It's game over! Why leave us alone now?"

He leaned back against the bars. "Amon has been trying to catch Kade for quite some time, and I'm sure he'll have his idea of fun with him before he comes back for us."

Oh God, she thought. She didn't even want to imagine what "fun" meant to an evil angel. Still, she felt compelled to ask. "What exactly will he do to him?"

"Torture, of course."

Samuel said it so casually that it made her want to punch him in the face. After all that Kade had done for her, this was how it ended. With her stuck in chains, helpless to get to him. She felt worthless. Worse, Samuel didn't even seem to care, and she wondered what kind of a monster could be that cold.

"Not a monster. Angel. Remember? And I'm not worried for two reasons: one, I can't do anything about it right now."

He held up his chained wrists, waving them around to prove the point; "And two, Amon knows how much Kade means to me. If he's planning to kill him, he'll wait and force me to watch."

The brain invasion was uncomfortable, and she flinched. "I thought we already established that it's rude to invade my thoughts? Remember?"

Samuel smiled at her quick tongue. "That time, it was necessary. You need to try and keep a clear head for what's to come. I know it's not easy to accept that Kade will have to endure any kind of pain, but at least he will stay alive. For now."

Ava was on the verge of hysterics just thinking about losing Kade, and in that moment, she realized she loved him. Inwardly, she cursed herself for being too afraid to tell him. Grief turned to rage, and she began pulling on her chains. "You really can't get us out of these?"

He pulled tightly on his chains in response. "I've tried everything I can think of since Amon brought me here. I don't know what spell he used, but I can't break it. Do you see the symbols carved into the steel bars around us?"

Looking around, she couldn't believe she hadn't noticed them earlier. They were everywhere, glowing with a strange yellow light. The symbols looked like a triquetra, but instead of having three intertwining ovals, these had five.

Samuel interrupted her thoughts. "It's a containment spell of some kind, mixed with something else that tampers down my powers. I don't know where Amon learned it, but the only other place I've seen anything like this was in Heaven."

Feeling defeated, she pulled her knees up to her chest and wrapped her arms around them. Then, they were facing each other, she and her birth father. Talk about weird. "I don't really know what to say to you."

Smiling at her, he said, "You don't have to say anything. You can't begin to understand how amazing it is to finally see you in person again after all this time. I've watched over you your whole life, but having you with me again, even under these circumstances, is just. Honestly, I have no words!"

She felt the sincerity in his voice and wanted to reciprocate the sentiment, but this wasn't how she'd ever envisioned meeting her birth father. Instead, she asked him a stupid question, "Kade said you could only come to Earth for one year every hundred, is that true?"

"Yes. If you hadn't ended up here, we would have never met. By the time I'm allowed back to Earth, you'll be gone. I take that back."

She was so sick of everyone being cryptic. "Explain?"

Crossing his arms over his broad chest, he said, "You're the only half breed that's ever existed. Well, the only one that I know of. We already know you have some of my powers, so it's reasonable to think that your life span might be different from a regular human. So far, you've grown like a normal human child, but only time will tell."

Ava couldn't imagine outliving everyone she loved. Just thinking about it caused the panic to rise again inside her chest. According to Samuel, if she managed to survive this whole ordeal, she would have some serious PTSD issues for the rest of her life, which could be extremely long. After taking a few deep breaths, she managed to calm down a little. Reminding herself again that she needed to have a clear head now and could officially lose her shit later, like after they averted the apocalypse.

"Why did Amon bring us here? What exactly does he want?"

Sighing, Samuel said, "Didn't Kade tell you what happens if he gets back into Heaven?"

Nodding, she said, "Yes, but I want to hear it from you."

"As soon as Amon escaped his holding cell, he began absorbing souls in the hopes of becoming strong enough to escape Purgatory. If he did find a way out, he could flash straight into Heaven. Purgatory negates his powers, so he is stuck here for now. He brought me here to absorb my powers too, but it's a much slower process. I feel the spell draining them out of me, but I'm stronger than any soul, and I've been fighting it the best I can. The longer the process goes on, the more of me he takes in. One of my powers is the ability to send souls to Heaven or Hell. So, when he finally takes all my power, he won't have to worry about getting out through the portal because he will be able to flash himself straight to Heaven."

"How can the other souls get out of the portal if he can't?" she asked.

Samuel was quiet for a moment before he answered. "I have a few theories on that. Since all the souls in Purgatory were once tied to Earth, in human bodies, maybe they were always able to travel back and forth. Before your mother was killed, I'd never been made aware that any shadows could do that or even thought about it. Or maybe, the shadows themselves didn't know they could leave until Amon started using them. Honestly, I don't know."

Resting her head against the bars of the cell, she wondered what Amon's end game was. "If Amon is so evil, why does he want to get back into Heaven anyway?"

Snapping his head up, Samuel pegged her with an intense stare. "Evil is the reason, Ava. He is so corrupted by vengeance and hate that he wants nothing more than to start the apocalypse. He was cast out like the rest of us and then stuck in a holding pit to rot for his crimes. He wants to take his revenge against God, and what better way to do it than by jump-starting the apocalypse?"

An evil angel with nothing to lose. Great, she thought, just great. "Even if it means destroying himself in the process?"

Fidgeting against his chains again, he answered, "Yes!"

She sighed, staring at her father. "Did you even care that one day I might develop powers I wouldn't understand? If I'd never come here, how would I have known what was happening to me? Especially if I stop aging? You've seen what the world is like. If I started doing things uncontrollably, the government would have put me in a lab somewhere, never to be seen again!"

He stopped fidgeting, focusing all his attention on her. "I would have done everything in my power to help you. Luckily, you found out before that happened."

She knew she was being hard on him and decided to change the subject. "Can you tell me about my mother?"

His entire face lit up as he answered. "Her name was Emmie, and she was the most beautiful woman I've ever seen. And that's saying something, considering I've been around since it all began. Most of the time, when I visit Earth, I flash around to all my favorite places to see how they've changed over the centuries. I was visiting the Florida Keys, about to board a diving boat, when I noticed your mother and her friend sitting outside at an open-air restaurant having dinner. I couldn't help myself and walked right up to her, rudely interrupted their conversation, and asked if I could buy her a drink. I thought she'd slap me, but instead, she accepted, and that was that. It was love at first sight, and she was pregnant with you in no time flat. I was in shock for most of her pregnancy because I never thought it was possible to conceive a child with a mortal. Nine months later, you were born, and I got to spend almost a month with you before I had to leave. Emmie named you after her mother, and I'm glad your adoptive parents chose to keep your name."

He paused, looking out through the cage for a moment. "Leaving you both was the hardest thing I ever had to do. I never told Emmie I was an angel, and I knew when I left that she'd always wonder why, but I had no choice. Up until that moment, I'd never really minded my sentence here, but the second I walked out the front door, I would have given anything to stay. I prayed, I cursed, I begged, but God wasn't listening. I was sent back to Purgatory and stuck here when they killed her."

Pausing again, he took a deep, shuddering breath. "She died because of me, and I'll never forgive myself!"

Wanting to comfort him, she scooted as close to him as possible. She reached out for his hand, and when he took hers, bright white light poured out all around them, temporarily blinding her.

Samuel noticed the startled look on her face and patted her hand for reassurance. "Our powers are just reacting to each other."

Squinting, she tried to see him through the light.

"It's the purest of all light, Ava. All angels have it, and it's the source of our power."

He laid his other hand over their joined ones, and the light dimmed.

She desperately wanted to know how to do that. "Can you help me control it? So far, I've only been able to access it a few times, and most of them were in highly emotional situations. It would help if I could do it with a level head."

Absently, he rubbed his hands over hers. "I imagine it's different for you because you're human. The only advice I can give is to try to tap into your emotions when you need it."

"That's what Kade said!" she huffed, "But, it's easier said than done."

Samuel smiled again. This time, with pride. "Kade is a smart boy. You really do care for him, don't you?"

Ava felt a little embarrassed talking about her feelings with him but answered anyway. "I'm sure you already know exactly how I feel about him since you can read my mind, but yes, I do! He', he's, he's...I don't know! He's just him, and it's perfect!"

Lifting a brow, he said, "I imagine he feels the same way about you. He always seemed a little too eager to go watch over you."

It was her turn to smile.

"I'd like to do something for you if you'll let me?" Samuel asked.

Intrigued, she asked, "Depends on what it is."

"I can show you, my memories. Would you like to see what your mother looked like?"

Ava was nervous but jumped at the opportunity. This was the only time she would ever be able to see her mother. "Yes. Please!"

Lifting his hands, he placed them on both sides of her face. "Close your eyes. This might feel a little strange at first, but just go with it."

Nodding, she closed her eyes. With a slight jolt, the vision appeared in her mind. She was standing in a hospital room, surrounded by random machines beeping and chiming. The image came into focus as she walked further into the room. A white curtain divided the room, and when she pulled it back, she found a petite woman sitting in a hospital bed. She was shocked to see just how closely she resembled her mother. Samuel was right; it was like looking in a mirror. Except where she seemed plain, Emmie was anything but. She radiated feminine beauty with long, curly, brown hair that cascaded down around her perfect petite face. Her eyes were the same almond shape as Ava's but were hazel instead of black. She realized how hard it must be for Samuel to look at her when she looked so much like his Emmie. Speaking of

Emmie, she was busy staring down at the newborn baby in her arms, clearly overwhelmed with love. Ava could never thank Samuel enough for giving her this gift. The beautiful vision disappeared all too soon, and she was back in the filthy cage.

Samuel was still holding onto her face, wiping away her tears. "She always wanted to be a mother and was over the moon about you."

Sniffling, Ava said, "I wish I'd felt that kind of love all my life. If you've been watching, then I'm sure you know my adoptive parents are less than superb!"

Samuel shook his head in disappointment. "Your foster parents have provided for you as best they can. They are different from your mother and me, that's true, but they love you fiercely. Just because someone doesn't love you the way you want to be loved doesn't mean they don't love you at all."

She wasn't in the mood for a lecture on why she should appreciate her foster parents. Not when she'd just felt the kind of love that she longed for her whole life. She was exhausted, mentally, physically, and emotionally, and just wanted this all to be over. On top of it all, she still didn't understand how she could help Samuel, especially when they were both chained down inside a cage.

"What do I have to do with all of this anyway? If Amon just wants your powers, then why did he send the shadows to attack me, and why did you want Kade to bring me here if something happened to you?"

"After your mother was killed, I wasn't taking any chances with you. Up until now, I didn't think Amon knew about you, but I knew if he found out, he would use you to get to me. To this day, apart from Kade, I never told anyone about you. I can only assume the shadows have been following you since you were a baby, and Amon was just biding his time. I told Kade to bring you here if anything happened to me because if I'm unable to use my powers or Amon takes them, I wouldn't be able to send him to watch over you. I'd rather have you here, with him to protect you, than on Earth, alone. Being the paranoid parent I am, I was always worried someone or something would take you away from me. After discovering that Amon was plotting against me, I hoped you had developed some powers and could help me if the time came. It was a long shot, but it seems I was right on all accounts. Now, I think Amon planned to bring you here all along as a fail-safe. If he gets all my powers and still can't get into Heaven for some reason, then he will try to take yours to double his chances."

Abruptly, Samuel stopped talking, his eyes darting outside the cage. "I need you to be strong now; Amon's coming!"

Chapter 27

At first, Ava didn't see anyone or hear anything, so she assumed superhuman hearing was one of Samuel's many powers. Then, she heard the footsteps. The pounding steps mimicked her frantic heartbeat, vibrating the floor as they got closer. The footsteps were accompanied by another strange noise. It sounded like something significant was being hauled across the floor. When Amon finally appeared in front of the cage, she didn't even register what he looked like. All she could focus on was Kade's limp body that was being dragged over the ground like trash. Kade's clothes were torn to shreds, and he was covered in blood. Thankfully, she could still see a slight rise and fall in his chest.

Looking up, she finally saw him. Amon. He was handsome. Very handsome. For some reason, she'd expected him to look hideous, but then again, evil rarely showed its true nature. Amon looked a lot like Samuel.

Only his eyes were ice blue instead of black. He was wearing black combat fatigues, with an array of weapons strapped to his legs and chest. His huge black glossy wings sprouted up and out of his back. At almost twice his size, the wings engulfed the entire hallway. The tips brushed against the ceiling while the rest dragged behind him on the dirty floor. When he looked at her, he smiled, flashing a mouth full of sharp pointed teeth. The sinister smile made her skin crawl. Then she saw it. Something dark was hovering just below the surface of his skin, making his attractive human features look like a mask. Focusing more on his face, she found his beautiful blue eyes to be dead and cold. The two things combined made his otherwise handsome face morph into something evil.

"Well, look at this. What a sweet family reunion!"

He taunted in a deep and raspy voice. Grabbing onto the bars with both hands, he stared at Ava. "Mmmm! She's a pretty one, isn't she?"

She tried to scoot even closer to Samuel, but the chains prevented it.

"Stay away from her!" Samuel snapped in a gravelly voice that sounded more animal than human.

"Or what?" Amon laughed, "What are you going to do chained to the floor like a dog? It's finally time you learned your place."

With a flick of his wrist, both of Samuel's legs snapped backward. Screaming in pain, he fell over onto his side. Swinging open the cage door, Amon stalked inside towards her. Unable to help, Samuel laid on the floor, panting as his bones snapped back into place. Amon walked over and crouched down in front of her. Refusing to look at him, she started over to where Kade's body was lying in the hallway. Amon grabbed her chin roughly, bringing her face up to look at his. When he did, his horrid breath fanned out over her nose and mouth. She gagged.

"Pretty! But so stupid!" he mocked.

"Let go of me!" she snapped.

Amon dropped his hand and wiped it off on his pants like he was disgusted from touching her. "Stupid and mouthy! I hope you and Daddy had some good quality time together because it's time to finish this."

With a snap of his fingers and they were instantly transported out of the cage and into a dungeon of some kind. Samuel was still chained, but he was hanging by his hands from the ceiling this time, while Kade's limp body lay sprawled in an awkward position in the corner. Ava fared far worse as her hands and feet were strapped down on a long table metal table. Next to the table laid a tray full of bloody knives, syringes, and other kinds of weapons she'd never seen before. She looked over at Samuel, and his eyes were ablaze.

Amon was standing by the fireplace, swirling a metal rod in and out of the flames. When the poker began glowing red, he pulled it out and walked over to her. All the while, staring at Samuel with a smug look on his face,

"I've already broken your golden boy. Let's see how you like watching me torture her."

Without warning, Amon jammed the red-hot poker through her right shoulder. Burning pain blasted through her, and the entire room fuzzed out for a moment. When things came back into focus, her whole arm felt warm from the blood flowing down it. The chains holding Samuel rattled as he strained to break free, just as Amon stabbed her again, this time through the other shoulder.

"Stop!" Samuel screamed.

Amon laughed again. "Why would I stop? Are you going to give me the rest of your powers willingly?"

Samuel didn't respond.

"Didn't think so. But no worries, I'll suck you dry eventually." He spat. "You should have just given your powers to me when I first brought you here. Now, I just feel like making you watch while I tear her to pieces."

Amon returned his focus to her.

"Third time's the charm?" he asked as he struck her again. This time, right through the stomach. She heard the loud clink when the poker came out through her back and hit the metal table. Blinding agony racked through her entire body. Blanking out again, she saw Kade's face in her mind. Physically, she was ready to give up, but mentally, she refused to. Not yet. She had to fight for him! For herself! For Samuel! For everyone!

Her eyes began to gloss over, white spots flickering in and out of her line of vision. Right before she closed her eyes, she swore she saw a blur of movement in the corner, over by Kade's body. Or maybe not, she thought. Everything felt floaty and distant.

"When you get into Heaven, he'll destroy you!" Samuel yelled.

"Maybe? Maybe not? You know our kind never belonged on Earth, Samuel. No angel should have to live with those animals. Then there's you. He stuck you here and forced you into servitude. What did you do about it? Nothing! I'm surprised you didn't just bend over for him. You are weak and deserve what's coming to you. I'm tired of waiting for it all to end. I'd rather be amid war than be stuck here or on Earth any longer."

Walking back to the fireplace, Amon reheated the poker. She tried to look over at Samuel one last time, but her line of vision was blocked. Trying hard to focus, Ava was shocked to find Kade standing beside her. He put his index finger up to his mouth to make sure she didn't make a sound and placed both of his hands over her stomach. Her whole body tingled as Kade healed her. Then, he flashed right behind Amon, stabbing him in between his massive wings with one of the knives she'd seen on the tray. Unfazed, Amon swung around and backhanded him so hard that he flew across the room, slamming into the wall with a loud crack.

Amon took his time as he stalked toward Kade. "I'm so glad you're awake. Now I get to kill you while they both watch!"

Kade tried to get up off the floor but stumbled and fell back down, blood pouring out of his mouth and nose. Amon picked him up with one hand, lifting him in the air as he choked him. Kade punched and kicked repeatedly, but it was no use. Amon tightened his grip, and Kade's movements slowed.

Ava felt a weird tingle move through her head.

"Use your powers to try and break our chains!" It was Samuel's voice. A whisper inside her mind.

She looked over at him, trying to send a silent message back. *"How can I break them if you can't?"*

"I don't know, but if you don't try, Kade will die."

Kade's face was turning blue. They didn't have much time. She tried focusing all her energy as Kade and Samuel had taught her, but she was too scared to do anything but watch Amon strangle Kade.

Amon's face morphed from man to a beast just as he pulled a knife out of his chest holster and plunged it straight into Kade's heart.

Samuel screamed inside her head. *"Now Ava, do it NOW!"*

Laughing, Amon dropped Kade's lifeless body to the ground and kicked it. Her heart sank, grief and rage building up inside her. Kade was dead! DEAD! At that moment, she wanted nothing more than to wrap her hands around Amon's throat and send him to the same fate. All four chains holding her exploded at once as white light poured out from her body. She quickly jumped off the table, but Amon was faster, flashing directly in front of her before her feet even touched the ground. Smiling, he smacked her across the face so hard that she somersaulted backward over the table, landing on the ground, right next to Kade's body.

His once brilliant green eyes were now dull and lifeless. Ava sucked in a harsh breath, unable to accept that he was gone.

"Flash to me!"

Flash to him? What was he talking about? The only power she knew for sure she had was the crazy light show. While she had her inner debate, Amon grabbed the table separating them and flung it across the room.

"I guess you do have some of Daddy's powers. Interesting! I'll make sure to take them before I kill you."

Grabbing her by the hair, Amon dragged her towards the fireplace. She tried to fight him, but her powers weren't working anymore. Maybe she'd tapped them out by breaking the chains, or perhaps she was just too traumatized by seeing Kade's dead body to access them. Either way, this was the end. She prayed to whoever was listening that Samuel would find a way to stop Amon. If not, at least she wouldn't be alive to witness the end of the world. Her contemplating ended when Amon threw her against the wall. Hard! Then, he knelt in front of her and pressed his hands tightly against her skull, murmuring in the same language Kade had so many times before. Except when Amon did it, the words felt evil and disgusting. Her body jolted forward as he began to drain her powers. It felt like her soul was being torn from her body.

Amon closed his eyes, smiling in satisfaction. "So. Much. Power!"

His arms began to glow from the transfer.

"Ava, if he finishes, he will kill both of us. FLASH TO ME!"

Amon took one of his hands off her head, and with a flick of his wrist, another huge knife appeared in his other hand. "Almost done, pretty girl! Ready to meet our maker? Spoiler alert, he's a real asshole."

Amon still had one hand holding onto her head while he reared the other one back, ready to strike. As she watched him bring down his hand, everything went into slow motion. Ava saw the knife coming down towards her, slow, slow, slower. When it was about an inch above her heart, she lunged to the right and landed on her back, quickly rolling onto her stomach. Looking up, she saw that Amon hadn't moved. He was still crouched in the same position, with the knife in his hand. Only, she wasn't sitting there anymore.

"*COME TO ME!*" Samuel screamed inside her head, his words so loud they gave her a headache.

Ava bee-lined it across the room to where Samuel was still hanging.

"*What do I do?*" she projected back to him.

"*The same thing you did on the table.*"

Amon stood. "Nice trick. But guess what? I can do it too!"

Amon flashed in right in front of her. Terrified, Ava turned around and grabbed onto Samuel. When she touched him, white light shot out in a bright stream, fanning out all around them. She could feel what was left of Samuel's powers mixing with hers. It felt good, and it felt strong!

"Focus all our power on him. Picture the light consuming and destroying him."

Using all the pent-up fury, anger, and pain she had over Kade's death, she did as Samuel instructed, just as Amon reached out to grab her again. This time, when his hand touched her throat, it caught on fire, instantly burning to ash. Screaming in agony, Amon took a lumbered step backward, holding onto the stump with his other hand. His eyes were wide with shock as he looked from her to Samuel and then back again.

"Impossible!" he howled.

"Looks like someone might be watching over us after all," Samuel said out loud.

Invigorated by the power boost, Ava smiled, focusing all their combined energy on Amon again. This time, light exploded out from her entire body, covering him from head to toe. It crackled and sizzled all around him. He let out one loud blood-curdling scream, and then the room fell silent. When the light finally subsided, she and Samuel were alone, and Amon was gone.

Chapter 28

When Amon disappeared, the chains holding Samuel snapped open, and they both fell to the floor. Samuel pulled her into his arms. "I knew you could do it!"

Hugging him back, she looked up to find tears pooling in his dark eyes. Seeing him be so emotional opened a flood gate, and she began to cry as well. Through the tears, she managed to smile, taking comfort in the fact that Amon was gone. Her comfort was short-lived once she saw Kade's lifeless body lying on the other side of the room. The tears of joy quickly turned to cries of pain. She flashed over to him. This time, it was easy, as simple as breathing. Taking his big strong hands in hers, she noticed they were cold as ice. Why hadn't she found the strength to tell him how she felt before?

"Kade. My sweet Kade!" she whispered, brushing the bloody matted hair away from his face.

"I know you can't hear me, but I love you! Dammit, I should have told you before, but I was a coward." Her words cut off in between sobs. As she looked at his face, her heart broke into a thousand pieces.

Kade would never kiss her again, never hold her, never reassure her, or protect her. He was gone. A beautiful light snuffed out. She might have saved the world for everyone else, but her world was destroyed the moment he took his last breath.

Samuel's hand pressed gently onto her shoulder. "I'm going to flash us back to my castle."

"Wait! What about him? We can't just leave him here!" she demanded.

"Don't worry. I've got him too," Samuel said softly, just as Kade's body disappeared.

Closing her eyes, Ava leaned back into Samuel's arms and let him flash her back to the castle. This time, they were in a different part of the castle, and she was thankful for that. She didn't have the strength to walk by Kade's room again. They were standing in a vast room she assumed was the living room. Plush fur rugs were strewn here and there, and in the corner sat a large wooden pallet covered in leather. Samuel set her down on the pallet and used his powers to start a cool fire in the oversized mantel. That's when she got her first honest look at Samuel standing up. He was towering. Much taller than she had initially imagined and was now sporting his own set of enormous white wings. They were amazing!

Standing, she walked over to him and tentatively touched one. It was thick and downy soft. "How do you have wings now? I didn't see any before?"

Samuel smiled. "They were always there. It's just uncomfortable to have them out when I'm sitting down or chained to the ceiling. I can easily fold them into my back when needed."

He turned around to demonstrate, and sure enough, the wings began to shrink, tucking into two folds of skin right under his shoulder blades.

All she could manage was a, "Wow!"

Samuel walked to the other side of the room and sat in a huge ornate chair that looked more like a throne. The thing was massive, with large gold wings that jutted up towards the ceiling. The wings then fanned out to form the back of the chair itself.

Once Samuel was settled, she assaulted him with questions. "How was I able to break out of the chains if you couldn't?"

"I have two theories. One, since you are half-human, perhaps the spells Amon was using didn't work against you. Maybe your mixed blood has something to do with it. The other is simply that a higher power intervened."

Both of his theories made sense. Well, as much as anything made sense in this new crazy world of hers. The next question was harder for Ava to ask, "What did you do with Kade's body?"

Samuel hung his head low, clearly as upset about Kade as she was. "I flashed him to the basement where my guards will prepare him for a proper burial. Kade was a warrior and will receive a warrior's last rights."

Ava didn't know what that meant but wanted to be a part of it. "When will it happen?"

"Tonight. But, the second the ceremony is complete, I'm sending you home."

Suddenly overwhelmed with anxiety, she paled. How was she going to explain being gone to her parents? Samuel must have been rereading her mind because he cut in on her inner monolog. "That is the last thing you need to worry about right now, my sweet girl."

Rolling her eyes, she said, "How can I not worry?! They're going to kill me. Literally!!"

Samuel laughed loudly. "You're being dramatic! You've only been here for a short time and time moves differently in this place. It's not linear, so I can manipulate it easily. With my powers, I can send you back on Sunday morning. It will be like you never left.

Sunday. Her birthday, she thought. The day of the huge fight with her parents. The day the shadows tried to drown her in the bathtub. The last day of her so-called normal life.

Samuel continued, "I want you to be as much of a normal kid as possible. I don't know when this world might collide with yours again or if something worse will happen in the future. I was hoping to shelter you from this side of your life, but as you can see, sometimes things don't work out how we want them to. I can't guarantee that I won't need you again or that someone else,"

He pointed upwards. "Might call upon you. So, you must try to enjoy being a normal human being for as long as you can."

She was taken aback by his words. How could he possibly think she could ever go back to being a normal kid after everything they'd been through?

"Seriously?" she asked him. "How am I supposed to care about mundane teenage issues when we just saved the world? Going back to high school seems so insignificant."

Samuel sighed, "Ava, I would have given up being an angel for your mother if I could have. A human life is what you are meant to have. I truly believe that if your mother had known the truth about us, she still would have wanted a normal life for you. You did something amazing today, but it's time to go home!"

Feeling angry, she sat back down on the pallet. She'd just met Samuel and wasn't ready to leave him just yet. "My adopted parents don't care about me as much as you do! Why can't I stay for a little while and spend more time getting to know you? And, if you couldn't send Kade back, how do you know you can send me back?"

Samuel walked across the room, and sat down on the floor in front of the pallet. He was so tall. Even sitting on the floor, his head was higher than hers. "Those parents that you say don't care about you have been losing their minds looking for you. Let me show you!"

He pressed his hands against her temples, and she instantly saw flashes of everything that had happened on Earth since she'd been gone. She saw Gabe, terrified, running towards his car through the rain, where he frantically called the police. He'd been forced to lie to everyone, telling them she'd slipped off the dock in the rain. After what he'd been through with Holly, she couldn't blame him. It was hard for people to accept the unexplainable. Even after all the crazy things that had happened to her before she came through the portal, even she would never have believed it was real had she not ended up in Purgatory. Before seeing it with her own eyes, she would have chalked it all up to her imagination and seen a shrink. The night before she'd come here, she'd told her dad the very same thing and agreed to see a doctor. Human beings just weren't wired to handle that kind of information.

Next, she saw flashes of the police and people from the community scouring the lake for her. Images of her parents crying and holding onto each other. More flashes, this time of her parents putting up missing girl signs throughout the neighborhood. Even though the police told them it was hopeless, they refused to accept that she was gone and kept searching. Then she saw Liv, crying and holding a picture of her while watching T.V. footage of the search. The very last image was of Kat and her family. They had all flown out to Denver to help her parents. Her heart melted.

Samuel removed his hands, and the images slowly faded. "I think I just showed you the answer to your first question. As for the second, I'm not sure I can send you back, but I'm going to try!"

He picked up her hands and looked her straight in the eyes. "Do you understand now what I meant about love? You saw how they feel, Ava; the love is there. If you need more to feel it here," He pointed to her heart, "Then you have to be brave enough to tell them what you need. When you get back, promise me you'll tell them."

It was a hard truth, but one she knew was right. Over time, she'd built up a wall around her heart. Now, it was time to stop blaming her adoptive parents for all the wrong in their relationship and own her part of it. "I promise," she said and meant it.

Chapter 29

Samuel left Ava alone, saying he needed to prepare for the burial. Anxious, she wandered into the tiny bathroom on the far side of the living room to freshen up. Seeing her reflection in the mirror made her recoil. Her dark brown hair was matted with grease, and the dark blue-black circles under her eyes stood out against her pale skin, making her look sick and gaunt. Her clothes were ripped, soiled with sweat, and covered with dirt. But none of that compared to the horror she felt when she looked at her hands. They were covered in dark, dried blood. Kade's blood, she thought with a cringe.

Turning on the water in the sink, she made it as hot as possible. Sobbing, she scrubbed her hands until they were raw. After the water ran clear, she grabbed a towel and wiped her face off. There wasn't much she could do about her hair without shampoo, so she just dunked her head under the sink to wet it down. She was exhausted, mind, body, and soul.

When she stepped out of the bathroom, Samuel was waiting for her by the door. He was wearing a suit made of metallic plated armor. His jet-black hair was combed away from his face, and his eyes held a grim expression. He looked amazingly put together, which made her feel even more self-conscious about her appearance.

Samuel motioned for her to come over to him, and when she did, he pulled her in for a quick embrace. "I'm going to miss you!"

She was going to miss him too. He took a step back, looking her up and down. He didn't seem put off by her appearance, but compared to him, she looked awful.

Shrugging, she said, "I tried to clean up in the bathroom, but it is what it is."

He flicked out his wrist the same way she'd seen Amon do, and instantly she felt clean. Stunned, she ran back into the bathroom. This time, her reflection showed spotless attire and hair that was dry and silky smooth. Sadly, the dark circles under her eyes remained.

Tears filled her eyes again, and she reached out for Samuel's hand. "Thank you. I didn't want to look like a hot mess the last time I saw him."

Samuel nodded in understanding. "You're welcome. Are you ready?"

Sighing heavily, she followed him out the door. They were halfway down the hallway when two people came barreling out of a passageway beside them. Scared, she jumped behind Samuel.

"It's okay, Ava; these are my men."

She remembered Kade telling her about the "good souls" that worked for Samuel while trying to redeem themselves. Still, seeing them in person was a shock. The souls helping Amon had been dark masses of smoke, while these looked like ordinary people.

"How many are left?" She asked as they approached.

"Just these two," Samuel said, "I summoned them back to the castle when we arrived."

They were both dressed in armor, similar to Samuel's.

"Sir!" the one on the right said.

"Yes!" Samuel answered in an authoritative tone.

Lefty seemed nervous, yelling out, "Kade's body is gone! We went down to the basement to retrieve it for the burial, and it's not there!"

Samuel looked stunned. "Have you searched the entire castle?"

"Yes, sir, twice! There were no signs of a breach." Righty said.

"Do it again!" Samuel growled.

On his command, both guards spun around and ran down the hallway. Grabbing her by the arm, Samuel rushed them back into the living room. "I have to send you home now!"

"What... no!" she protested, "I want to say goodbye to Kade. I HAVE to say goodbye to him, please!" She was on the verge of hysterics.

Samuel calmed down and turned her to face him. "You already said goodbye to him, honey. Don't you remember? In the dungeon, before I flashed us here. You told him what was most important! I don't know what's going on, but I can't risk keeping you here any longer!"

"Please don't do this!" she pleaded.

Hugging her tightly, he said, "I love you too much to let anything happen to you. I couldn't protect your mother, and I won't make the same mistake twice!"

She wasn't ready to go but understood.

He kissed her on the forehead. "I love you, Ava. Never doubt that! If we never meet again, know that I'm always watching!"

His familiar eyes filled with tears and her heart broke all over again. "I love you too, Dad!"

He placed his hands on her temples. "This is going to hurt a little, but don't fight it."

"I trust you," she whispered, too choked up to speak any louder.

Her body began to vibrate, and she felt like she was being spun around on a Tilt-A-Whirl. Faster and faster, she turned, until everything in her line of vision blurred into darkness. Then, it felt like she was being pulled backward. The pressure of the pulling, mixed with the vibrating and spinning, made her head feel like it was going to explode. The sensations only lasted for a few seconds, and when everything stopped moving, she was sitting on her bed. IN HER ROOM! The curtains were closed, but she could tell it was still dark outside. Looking over at the clock, it read 3:00 AM.

Everything in her bedroom was as she'd left it—everything except her. The urge to wake up her parents and tell them the entire story was overwhelming. But to them, nothing had changed. None of the visions Samuel showed her had occurred. Or had they? Maybe they were going down an alternate timeline now. To be honest, she had no idea; the whole concept of time travel was ridiculous and confusing. Either way, her parents had no memories of her being gone, and even if they did, she could never tell them the truth. Just thinking about it all made her head spin. Laying down on her bed, she was bombarded with thoughts about Kade. Exhausted and feeling more alone than she ever had before, she quietly cried herself to sleep.

Chapter 30

The annoying beep of her alarm clock woke her a few hours later. Pounding on the snooze button, she wondered why the stupid thing was going off in the first place. It was Sunday. Thank God for that, she thought. She wasn't ready to face anything, let alone school. Just thinking about all her boring classes was enough to make her pull the covers back over her head. When the stupid alarm beeped a second time, she grabbed it, and ripped it from the wall, and threw it across the room. Frustrated, she laid back down in bed, obsessing about everything. Mainly about how she was supposed to go back to acting like a normal teenager when everything about her was so abnormal. Monsters were real. Angels were real. Heaven, Hell, Purgatory. ALL real. When she met Samuel, she'd planned to ask him if he'd been the one who created all the monsters in Purgatory. But she never got around to it. Now, after spending time with him, she knew the answer without question. There was no way Samuel was capable of creating such evil. He was a good man, or angel, or whatever. Staring at the ceiling, she wondered if she would ever get to see him again.

All the things Samuel had told her about her powers, as well as her potential life span, were just a wait-and-see kind of thing. It was terrifying to think about going on with her normal life when some new power could manifest itself at any moment. What would she do if she was having dinner with her parents and suddenly turned invisible? Or what if she lost control of her flashing ability and flashed out in the middle of a class? The potential for disaster was imminent. Then, she would be kidnapped by the CIA and sent to a lab somewhere. As if that wasn't bad enough, her main fear was the aging issue. If she stopped aging, how long would it take before other people noticed? Five years, ten? She had no idea, but just thinking about all the terrifying possibilities made her feel anxious and sick to her stomach. Adding insult to injury, a picture of Kade's face flashed through her mind again. Groaning, she forced herself out of bed, needing a distraction before a debilitating depression took hold of her. As if on cue, her mom walked into the room.

"Good Morning, birthday girl. It's time to get up!"

Talk about Déjà vu. "Morning, Mom!" Even though she knew what her mom was going to say next, she didn't cut in.

Her mom danced around the room again, opening curtains, and fluffing them. "Your Dad and I both made sure we were off today, so we can do anything you want."

Her hair still felt clean from Samuel's magic trick, but she hadn't officially showered in; oh wow, she couldn't even remember how long.

Forcing a smile, she said, "I'd really like to shower before making any important life decisions. Can you give me a few minutes to clean up?"

"Sure thing, honey. I'm making breakfast, so just come down when you're ready, and we can plan the day!"

Smiling, Ava softened a bit. Seeing her parents so distraught in Samuel's visions made her feel more empathetic towards them. Remembering her promise to Samuel, she stood up and hugged her mom tightly before she walked out the door. Her mom stiffened for a moment, probably stunned by her offer of affection, but then gently hugged her back.

Lumbering into the bathroom, she hesitated in the doorway when her eyes fell on the bathtub. The last time she'd been in there, the shadows had tried to drown her. She wanted to remind herself that Amon was gone and there was nothing to be afraid of, but that was easier said than done. After the water warmed up, she stepped inside the shower. It was Heaven, well, not literally, but Ava imagined that if Heaven really did exist, there would be amazing showers there. Letting the warm water soothe her tired body, she tried to relax and enjoy the moment. One minute turned to several, and when the water ran cold, she stayed under the spray, paralyzed, as her mind relived everything from Purgatory. The hard knock at the door startled her back to reality.

"Is everything okay?" her mom called out, "You've been in there for forty-five minutes."

No, everything was so not okay! She thought, not after losing Kade. It didn't feel right celebrating her life when he was gone.

Turning off the shower, she answered, "I'm not feeling well. Can we please postpone the birthday celebration until next weekend? I know you and Dad went through a lot to get off today, but I just want to rest."

She felt horrible lying to her mom, but there was no way she could fake happiness today.

Sighing, her mom said, "Of course, baby. Why don't you go back to bed for a while and we can try and have some cake later? I ordered your favorite cheesecake and everything."

"Thank you, Mom."

Ava never made it to the cake. After keeping busy most of the morning, quietly cleaning and organizing, she finally fell back asleep. What she thought would be a quick nap turned into a marathon of sleep that lasted until the following day. Luckily, she woke up in time for school since her alarm clock was still lying on the floor, unplugged. Still, she had to scramble to get dressed and out the door in time to meet Liv. As she whizzed by the kitchen, she saw her birthday cake sitting out on the table with a note taped to the top of the box. It was in her dad's handwriting.

Happy belated birthday. I came in twice yesterday, and you were sound asleep both times. You must be sick if you missed cake and slept for an entire day! I hope you're feeling better. You have our permission to stay home today if you need to. BUT, be warned, we are taking you to the doctor asap. Love, your worried Dad!

Ava considered taking her parents up on the offer to stay home until she realized that would only leave her with more time to think. Right now, thinking was the enemy. The frigid air assaulted her when she walked outside, and for once, she embraced it. After dealing with the sweltering heat of Purgatory, the cold air felt nice on her skin. Liv was already walking down the driveway when she arrived at her house.

Liv was a morning person, already bubbly and smiling. "Morning, girl!"

Seeing Liv smile warmed her heart, and instead of saying hello, she pulled her in for a tight bear hug.

Giggling, Liv said, "Well, hello to you too! How was your birthday? I left you like a bajillion messages, but you never called back!"

Shrugging, she said, "I'm sorry Liv, I've been feeling sick ever since we left the lake on Saturday and pretty much slept all day. I haven't even checked my phone messages yet. I'm hoping to have a birthday redo next weekend. Are you free? I won't be grounded anymore by then."

Liv smirked. "Of course! I'm always free for you. I'm glad you're feeling better now. I mean, you are feeling better? Right? Your parents aren't like forcing you to go to school sick for fear of you getting a B? Right? RIGHT?"

Now it was her turn to laugh, "No. For once, they're being cool. I still don't feel like myself, but I think I can manage school."

As they walked, she contemplated telling Liv everything. Liv was such a good listener and an even better secret keeper. But then she remembered how crazy it all sounded. Even if Liv wanted to believe her, she probably wouldn't be able to. The whole thing was just so far-fetched. Maybe she could tell it to Gabe? Not in a this really happened kind of way, but more like a, I've been thinking of this incredible story idea way. She knew he wrote his own comics and thought he might be able to turn her story into one. At least that way, she'd be able to talk about it with someone.

School turned out to be more of a challenge than she anticipated. Most of her classes now bored her to death. The only one she was mildly interested in was Greek Mythology, and that was only because, at this point, it was closer to her reality than any other subject. At lunch, she spied Gabe, Holly, Adam, Haven, and Megan all sitting around the table. Smiling, she waved to them all, even flashing Megan a genuine smile. A young, rude, mean girl was nothing compared to the real evil that existed out there. Looking at Gabe made her heartbreak a little. The last time he would remember seeing her was when they rushed home from the lake last Saturday. But her last memory of him was very different. His terrified face was the last thing she'd seen as she was pulled under the water. At least he didn't remember it now.

    The last time she'd seen Holly, she'd been pushing her for a picture of Kade. At the time, the poor girl probably thought she was mental. Now, that encounter had been erased as well. Ava was genuinely grateful to Samuel for setting her back in time. Her friends didn't need to know the kind of horrors that were out there if they didn't have to. Unfortunately, she would never forget. Haven eyed her wearily from across the table. Too bad the incident at the lake couldn't be erased. For now, she decided to play dumb and hoped Haven would never bring it up again. Thinking back on it, she still wasn't sure if the shadows had somehow possessed Haven that day or if the girl indeed was a witch. If angels and monsters existed, then why not witches? In fact, how many other things were out there that she didn't know about. She gulped nervously, just thinking about it.

The rest of the day passed by quickly, and by the end, she was anxious to get home. Tonight, she planned to talk to her parents about everything, including her adoption. It was going to be a hard conversation, but she was ready to move forward, which meant a fresh start. At this point, her parents were all she had left.

Once she got home, she decided to check her messages. Sure enough, there were several from Liv, and ten from Kat, ranging from excited to annoyed. She made a mental note to email Kat later. There was no way she could hear her voice right now without breaking down. She could never hide her real feelings from Kat, no matter how hard she tried. Trying not to think about sad thoughts, she busied herself with homework while waiting for her parents to come home. When she finally heard the front door open, she ran into the living room, practically tackling her dad with a hug.

Smiling, he stepped back to steady himself and then hugged her back. "Is everything alright?"

"Yeah, Dad. I'm just happy to see you. Sorry, I missed you yesterday."

Kissing the top of her head, he said, "Yeah, me too! And just so you know, I went ahead and made that doctor's appointment for you, and it's on Wednesday. How are you feeling now?"

There was no way she was getting out of going to the appointment, so she just played along. "I'm feeling a little better, but I think I should still go in and have a look-see. I mean, when was the last time I went to the doctor anyway?"

Her nightmares were gone, and she knew for sure she wasn't crazy, but convincing her parents of that was another story.

Her dad nodded. "Agreed!"

While she had her dad's attention, she knew it was time to ask for a family meeting. Talking was the first step to a better relationship, but she was still nervous about a sit-down. Following him into the kitchen, she paced around uncomfortably while he made a sandwich. After a lot of stalling, she finally asked, "Do you know what time mom will be home tonight?"

Shrugging, he said, "Probably around eight. They had to do a lighting test in the gallery tonight."

"Well, I want to talk to you both about some stuff tonight if you have time?"

He looked at her questioningly. "Okay, sure. But if there's something you need to talk about right now, we can!"

Walking out of the kitchen, she said, "Thanks but no thanks. I'd rather talk when you're both here. I'm going to go finish my homework, but please come get me when she gets home."

Chapter 31

Ava heard the front door open at eight-thirty. Twenty agonizing minutes later, there was a soft knock on her bedroom door.

"Come in!" she called out, as casually as possible.

It was her mom, "Dad called and filled me in on the request for a family meeting. Are you ready now? I picked up sushi!"

Her stomach growled in response. "I'm always ready for sushi!"

When they walked into the dining room, her dad was busy setting the table, and after the food was divided up, her parents looked over at her expectantly. Looking back at them, she recalled the day she found out she was adopted. She'd been five. During the first week of kindergarten, everyone in the class was assigned to bring in a family photo for a show and tell. That day, she noticed that most of the other kids looked like at least one of their parents. Confused as to why she didn't, she'd come home asking why. It would have been easy for them to lie, but instead, they chose that moment to tell her. At the time, she'd been too young to ask questions, and since then, she'd been too scared. Having heard Samuel's side of the story, she now wanted to know theirs.

Ava was having a hard time finding the right words to start the conversation. So instead of talking, she just sat in silence for a few minutes, pushing a tuna roll around her plate.

Finding her voice was hard, but she didn't want to be a coward anymore. "Look, I've never really had the nerve to ask you guys this before, but what do you know about my birth parents?"

They cast nervous looks at each other, and then it was her mom who spoke up first. "This conversation has been a long time coming. I'm sorry we didn't offer the information freely, but we wanted to wait until you were ready. We figured when you were, you'd ask, and I guess we figured right."

Her mom took her dad's hand in hers before speaking again. "I'm sorry, Ava, this is a tough subject for us too. We initially considered not telling you at all. But in the end, that didn't seem fair. That day you came home from school, you were just so confused, and well, we just..."

Tears pooling in her eyes, she continued, "We just hoped we would be enough. I know it's selfish, but a small part of me wished you would never ask. To us, it never mattered where you came from. You've always been ours! Your dad and I couldn't have children of our own. We tried for years and years, and it never happened. We were about to give up on the idea completely until one day, when I was driving home from work; I overheard a news report on the radio about adoption. We'd never even considered adoption up until that point. The next day, I contacted several agencies in town and finally found one we felt comfortable with. When we went in for our initial meeting, they explained the process to us, and we're confident something would work in the next few years. We got the call three days later about you. Normally, that doesn't happen. The agency told us your mother had passed away, and there was no family left to claim you. Since our agent liked us so much, she bypassed the waiting list and let us adopt you. The minute we saw you, we knew you were meant to be our daughter. When I held you in my arms for the first time, it felt so right!"

Now, it was Ava's turn to tear up.

"We know your birth mother passed away, but the agency didn't have any information on your father. The only thing they gave us was a few pictures. I saved them for you."

Her mom reached out, taking Ava's hand in hers. "I'm sorry, baby, but that's all we know."

Emotions running high, she was afraid to get into the other part of why she'd wanted this meeting. But it was now or never. Taking a deep breath, she pushed through the fear to tell them the truth.

"Listening to that story made me feel love from you. To be honest, I haven't felt much of it since I was a little kid. I know you mean well, but I feel like all I ever get from you are expectations, when all I've ever wanted is attention and quality time as a family. I feel like you always put work first, second, and third, and then there's nothing left for me."

Her dad was the one to speak up this time, "Of course, we love you! Your mom and I only work as hard as we do so that we can save money for your college fund. We never intentionally put work first, but we want you to have every opportunity in life, and a good education is important."

"I know, Dad, but it's not everything. I need you both now! Once I graduate and start my adult life, I want you to be in it. If I left tomorrow for college, feeling how I do now, I might not ever come back or want a relationship with you. Is that what you want? To work all the time to send me to school, and that's it? I want to be your daughter, not just some stranger with a stellar degree!"

Now, they were all crying. Ava's dad stealthily wiped away his tears, not wanting her to see them before responding. "You know, you're right. We've all gotten caught up in our daily routines and haven't been paying attention for a while."

With that, her mom got up, walked around the table, and hugged her so tightly she thought she might pop.

"What can we do to make it better?" her mom asked.

The only thing she wanted was more time with them. "To start, can you both try and be home more often for family dinner? I mean, I'm sick of heating up leftovers and eating alone."

Her mom hugged her even tighter if that was possible. "Of course, we can, baby! We will figure something out!"

After dinner and a lot more hugging, Ava asked to see the adoption agency's pictures. While she sat on the couch, waiting for them to come back in, she wished she'd talked to them sooner. Keeping her feelings to herself was an ongoing bad habit. One that she desperately needed to break. If she'd only had the courage to tell them years ago, who knows what might have been. For some reason, she always held things in, too afraid to speak her truth. To this day, she wasn't sure why. Maybe fear of rejection? In the end, all it did was prolong and magnify her problems. In Kade's case, it denied her the opportunity to tell him how she truly felt. Moving forward, she vowed to never hold back her true feelings again.

When her parents came back into the living room, her mom held a small brown box and gently set it down on the coffee table in front of her. "That's everything. The agency told us that most of the things in your mother's house were sold through escrow to pay off the mortgage. Thankfully, the police were thoughtful enough to save these photos, providing them to the agency for you."

Quickly popping off the lid, she sifted through the contents. There was a ton of legal paperwork spelling out the terms of the adoption. In the documents, she noticed Emmie's full name was listed as Emmalyn Marie Wescott. Emmalyn! Her adopted mom's name was Lynne. Kismet?

Maybe? At the very bottom of the box, there was a sealed manila envelope.

Looking up at her parents, she asked, "You never opened these?"

Her mom shook her head. "They're not for us. If you want to share them, you can. If not, that's okay too. We're going to go clean up and give you some alone time with them."

Realizing that sharing this moment with them would be another stepping stone, she asked, "Can you please stay?"

Her parents nodded, sitting down next to her on the couch. As soon as they did, she ripped the seal off the envelope, pulling out a handful of old photographs. The first few were of Emmie while she was still pregnant. They were all taken on a white sandy beach. Must be in Key West, she thought. In every photo, Emmie had her hands lovingly wrapped around her swollen belly, her long auburn curls blowing in the wind. Samuel must have taken them, she thought with pride.

The rest of the photos were of a familiar scene. They were all taken in the hospital room Samuel had shown her in the vision. She was thankful to have this permanent reminder of Samuel and Emmie, not that she would ever forget them. At that moment, she realized just how lucky she was. While most people only got one set of parents, she'd been blessed with two sets that truly loved her. Handing the photographs over to her mom, she waited for their reaction. Both of her parents looked them over and were taken aback by how much she looked like Emmie.

After a lot more tears and group hugs, she decided it was time for bed. Emotionally drained, she wanted nothing more than to close her eyes. After changing into her favorite pajamas, she laid down, proud that she was keeping her promise to Samuel, and for the first time in a long time, she fell asleep, looking forward to a new day and a new start.

Chapter 32

Ava's parents were trying hard to keep their word and managed to make it home in time for family dinner again on Tuesday. It was a nice change—a needed one. School, on the other hand, was the same ole, same ole. On Wednesday,

Haven stopped her in the hallway to talk. Luckily, it wasn't about the incident at the lake. Instead, she just asked her a bunch of questions about their mythology homework. They would probably never be besties after the episode, but at least Haven wasn't asking a bunch of questions she couldn't or wouldn't answer.

Things seemed to be getting back to normal, and thankfully, she hadn't sprouted wings or developed any other crazy abilities over the last few days. Since leaving Purgatory, she hadn't even tried to use her powers. For one, she didn't need them for anything on Earth, even though flashing was super fun. And two, she was afraid if she did use them, it might jump-start her metamorphosis or draw attention to herself. Her doctor's appointment Wednesday morning had turned out as expected. She was healthy as a horse. The doctor chalked all her problems up to stress and advised her parents to bring her back in if the nightmares started again. She'd also caught up with Kat a few times over the phone but always kept the conversations short. Every time she heard Kat's melodic voice, she felt compelled to come clean. The sad truth was, only two people would ever know her story. One of them was dead, and there was a good chance she would never see the other again. Three people saved the world, and no one would ever know. The solitude of keeping it to herself was hard, but even if she did tell someone, who would believe her?

Missing Kade proved to be even more difficult than keeping secrets. Every time she thought about him, she experienced a mini breakdown. Ava tried to reserve the crying fits for when she was alone in her room, but her parents were on to her. When they'd questioned her about it, she chalked it up to PMS and hormones. That answer seemed to appease them for now, but she knew if she didn't get her shit together soon, they were going to push harder. It wasn't like her to get emotional, like ever.

"Miss Chase!" Mr. White yelled, "Would you like to join us? Or would you like to continue your daydreaming in detention?"

"Hmm...What?" she asked, abruptly pulled from her thoughts.

Mr. White cleared his throat. "I asked you to come up and complete the equation on the blackboard."

"Oh!! Sorry!" she stammered. Completely lost in thought, she hadn't even heard him talking. Luckily, it was an equation she knew how to solve. After scribbling out the answer, she looked over at Mr. White expectantly. Nodding in satisfaction, he called on another student to complete the next one.

After class, Liv caught up with her in the hallway. "Hey, girl. Are you feeling okay today?"

Shrugging, she said, "Yeah, I'm good. I just have a lot on my mind, I guess."

Liv sighed. "You've been really distant over the past few days. You know I'm always here if you want to talk, right?"

"I do. Thanks, Olivia!"

Liv scrunched up her nose at her use of her full name. "Eww! You know I HATE being called that!"

Laughing, she lightly patted her on the arm. "Duh! That's why I do it! But, seriously, I'm fine. It's been an intense couple of days with my parents. P.S. you're a great friend for checking in on me."

Liv seemed to relax a little, changing the subject. "So, do you still want to hang out this weekend for the birthday do-over?"

Crap, Ava thought. She'd forgotten all about that.

She still didn't feel much like celebrating but hanging out with her friends for the day would be a nice distraction. "Yes! That sounds nice. Do you mind if we invite Gabe and Holly?"

"Of course not! It's your birthday celebration, so you can invite anyone you want. What do you want to do?"

The answer instantly popped into her head. "Why don't we have a re-do of our picnic at Devil's Head Lake? I still feel horrible for cutting it short last time."

Liv smiled. "I think that's a great idea, as long as you don't ralph again!"

"I can't guarantee it won't happen again. But if it does, I'll aim for your shoes!" Ava joked.

"By the way," Liv said, "Did you hear about the new guy?"

Ava shook her head. She'd barely noticed her friends the past few days, let alone some new person.

Now it was Liv's turn to be funny. "I haven't met him yet, but if he's as hot as everyone's been saying, Gabe might have some competition."

Adam and Gabe were already sitting at the table when they arrived in the lunchroom. There was also a third guy sitting with them, but she couldn't distinguish who it was because he was facing the opposite direction. Many of Adam's teammates stopped by to talk shop with him during lunch, so Ava didn't think anything of it. Right before she sat down at the table, guy number three turned around and locked eyes with her. Her whole body went numb, the lunch tray slipping from her hand, landing on the floor with a loud bang. Everyone turned to stare in her direction. Usually, being the center of attention would send her into a panic attack, but she didn't care right now. Nothing could pull her attention away from Kade's brilliant green eyes. He picked up the tray, placed it on the table, and then offered his hand to her.

Winking, he said, "You must be Ava?"

Chapter 33

Somehow, Ava's confused brain reconnected with her body enough that she managed an awkward handshake. The new guy was Kade.

"Ava, are you okay, Ava? You look like you just saw a ghost!" Gabe chuckled.

Gabe was right, though; she was looking at a dead person. In fact, she wondered why she was the only one freaking out. Everyone else thought he'd drowned years ago.

"Yeah, you don't look so good." Kade concurred. "Maybe you should go see the nurse."

She just nodded, unable to form words.

"I'll take her!" Liv volunteered.

"Can I take her? I mean, I startled her half to death and wouldn't feel right if I didn't do something. Is that alright with you, Ava?" Ghost Kade asked.

Dumfounded, Ava just nodded again.

Liv looked at him suspiciously but didn't argue.

Once they were alone, Kade backed her into a locker and kissed the breath out of her. "I missed that," he said with a huge grin.

Mind reeling, Ava pushed him away. "What in the hell is going on? I watched you die!"

In Purgatory, his body had disappeared from Samuel's castle, and no one knew why. What if a shadow or some other evil entity had taken it over and was walking around in Kade's skin. In her new world, the idea was plausible.

Still, the kiss felt like Kade.

"How do I know it's really you?"

Kade stepped away from her. "Ava, look at me! Really look! It's me!"

She wanted to believe him but, how could she? "You look like Kade, but that doesn't mean anything. Prove it!"

"Challenge accepted!" Without missing a beat, he recounted every nuance of their time together in Purgatory, including some things he'd witnessed while watching over her for Samuel. Embarrassing teenage things that she couldn't deny only he would know. Convinced it was him, she jumped into his arms and held on with everything she had.

"How?" she whispered.

"That's a story best left until after school," he answered.

"Okay! But, why isn't everyone else freaking out that you're back?"

"Samuel's not the only one with powers. Whoever sent me back has the power to change memories. As far as everyone else is concerned, I'm just the new kid."

Flashing her a cocky grin, he added, "Oh, and just in case you haven't heard, I'm totally a hottie!"

Rolling her eyes, she asked, "What about your family?"

His grin turned into a full-blown smile. "In their minds, we just moved to town. Whoever helped me managed to mind freak four years' worth of memories for an entire town. Even though I'm grateful, it's both incredible and scary to imagine something wielding that kind of power."

Her head was spinning. "Can we just leave now?"

Kade laughed, making her heart skip a beat. "No way! Skipping school on the first day is seriously frowned upon. Be patient. It's only a few hours until the end of the day."

"Still making me wait for answers!"

His smile widened. "Always!"

Kade kissed her once more before heading back into the lunchroom. Instead of following him, she went on to see the nurse in order to keep up appearances. When the final bell rang, she bee-lined it to the parking lot. Her last class of the day was on the total opposite side of the school, so it took her a good six minutes to get outside. Kade was already there, leaning up against Gabe's SUV, talking to him like the old friends they were. Kade looked over and, noticing her, said goodbye to Gabe. Her heart dropped into her stomach as she watched him stride across the parking lot towards her. He was just as handsome as ever. When he got close, she reached out to touch him, but he pulled away.

Seeing her confusion, Kade whispered, "We need to be a little discrete. All your friends think we just met like three hours ago."

She thought about it for a moment and then laughed. "Yeah, you're probably right. I can do discrete in public, but when we're alone, all bets are off!"

"Deal!" he agreed.

Liv came running up from behind them, clearly upset. "Ava! What's the deal? Were you just going to leave without me?"

Shit, she silently cursed. In all her excitement over Kade, she'd completely forgotten about Liv. She felt horrible, but having your dead boyfriend come back to life was enough to throw anyone off their A-Game. She tried to think of a good excuse, but none came to mind.

Instead, she went with a partial truth. "I'm so, so, sorry, Liv!! The episode at lunch made me look like a total loser, and I felt mortified. I was rushing home and blanked on waiting. Please don't be mad!"

Liv looked from her to Kade and then back again.

Clearing her throat, Ava said, "Oh, sorry again! Liv, this is Kade. Kade, this is my good friend Liv. He's the new guy you mentioned earlier."

Liv's face turned bright red. "I know. We officially met when he came back from taking you to the nurse."

The situation was awkward, and she didn't know what to do. Her story sounded pretty lame, considering she was with Kade and not walking home alone, and Liv was probably thinking the same.

Kade and Liv were both staring at her, so she only saw one option. "Cool. Well, do you mind if he walks with us today?"

"Does he even live near us?" Liv asked, eyeing him suspiciously.

Ava didn't have the answer. Thankfully, Kade chimed in and saved her. "Ava just told me what street she lives on, and I'm only a few blocks away. I still feel bad for being the cause of her nurse visit today and just wanted to make sure she got home okay."

After hearing his answer, some of Liv's annoyance vanished. "That's very thoughtful of you. You and Gabe seemed to hit it off pretty well?"

Kade nodded. "He's a pretty cool guy. I can't wait to see that room of his!"

Liv smiled. "Be prepared to be awed."

It warmed her heart to see them interact with each other. She hoped Liv grew to like him and vice versa.

They got to Liv's house in no time flat, and as she hugged her goodbye, Liv whispered, "We should plan a double date sometime soon. It looks like Mr. Hottie pants has a thing for you!"

Before she let Liv go, she whispered back, "Yeah, I think I like him too. Do you think I should invite him to the lake with us?"

Liv nodded, giggling as she walked up the driveway.

After Liv disappeared into her house, Ava didn't hesitate to question him. "Alright! I've waited all day! Spill!"

He took her hand in his. "Impatient as always! You're lucky I like that about you!"

He paused for a moment, stroking the back of her hand with his thumb. "This is our reward for saving the world. My life, for saving the lives of everyone else. I don't remember much, but while I was lying on the floor of that dungeon, there was this feeling of peace. I don't know if I went to Heaven or if it was God who sent me back, but there was some presence with me. All I know for sure is that whatever, or whoever it was, thanked me for my sacrifice and said I deserved another chance! It didn't speak to me with words, but somehow, I felt the meaning. Then, poof! I was back in my bedroom. Alive and well! It was all very confusing at first. I ran downstairs and found my parents in the middle of cooking dinner. When they saw me, they acted normal. That's when I knew their memories had been altered. After talking with them, I started to piece some of it together, but I still have to sift through four years of their new memories. Maybe you could come over and Q&A them for me."

He squeezed her hand tighter, tears pooling in his green eyes. "After all this time and everything that's happened, I can't believe I'm back on Earth!"

She couldn't imagine what it was like for him. She'd only been gone for a few days, and that felt like a lifetime. He'd been gone for years. Pulling him in for a hug, she realized she now had the opportunity to tell him how she felt. Without hesitation, she said, "I love you, Kade! I love you so much. I wanted to say it before, but I was too scared. And then...."

Ava paused, getting chocked up at the memory of his death. "Then, you were gone, and it was too late!"

Gently brushing the hair away from her face, he said, "I knew how you felt, even though you never said it. For the record, I love you too!"

Smiling, she kissed him passionately. He pulled back, ending the kiss far too soon and leaving her breathless. Standing at the front door, she motioned for him to come inside, but he didn't budge. Confused, she pulled on his arm. "Don't you want to come in?"

"Are your parent's home?"

"No, but they'll be here soon."

Taking a step back, he said, "Right, and I'm sure they'd be happy to find a strange boy alone in the house with you?"

She hadn't been thinking clearly all day. "You're right. They would freak out. We can just sit here on the porch and talk until they get home. I don't think they would mind us talking outside."

He smirked. "I don't want to start on the wrong foot with them. How about I go home for now? When they get here, you can tell them all about the new boy you met and how you invited him over for dinner tomorrow?"

That plan sounded good, except for the part where Kade had to be out of her sight. "I'm afraid if you leave, I'll wake up, and none of this will be real!"

He pulled her in for a tight embrace, "I promise that won't happen! Plus, I haven't seen my parents in so long."

Ava understood and reluctantly let him leave. Trying to keep herself occupied, she went inside and called Kat. She was excited to fill her in on the new guy news and glad she could finally be honest with her about something. By the time they got off the phone, her parents were home. Walking into the kitchen, she found her mom doing paperwork at the bar top table while her dad was busy changing out a light bulb above the sink. Trying to be as calm as possible, she pulled some yogurt and a spoon. As she ate, she casually mentioned meeting Kade, the lovely new boy who'd walked her home from school. Then nervously, she asked them if he could come over for dinner as a thank you. Shockingly, they agreed to it, as long she promised to finish her homework. Smiling, she felt on top for once.

Chapter 34

The next day, Kade met Ava in-between classes to talk. He even pulled her into an empty classroom during lunch to sneak in a kiss away from prying eyes. The PDA would have to wait a few more weeks until her friends got used to the idea of them dating. That afternoon, she walked home with Liv while Kade went home to change for dinner. After nailing down the details for the trip to Devils Head Lake the following day, she too went home to get ready.

Kade arrived promptly at seven. When she opened the door, he was holding a huge bouquet of white lilies.

"Wow, those are stunning!" she said.

Walking inside, he handed the flowers to her while he took off his jacket. He was wearing dark blue slacks and a long-sleeve button-down shirt. She wasn't used to seeing him dressed up, but it was a good look.

Smiling, he snatched the flowers back from her. "I'm glad you like them, but they're not for you!"

"Beg your pardon?" she asked, brow raised.

"They're for your Mom." he said with a smirk.

Laughing, she said, "Oh, I get it! You're schmoozing!"

Slipping her a quick kiss on the cheek, he said, "I got to do what I got to do."

Palms sweating, she walked him into the kitchen to meet her parents.

"Mom, Dad," she called out, trying to keep her voice even, "This is Kade. Kade, this is my mom, Lynne, and my dad, Daniel."

Her mom's eyes widened as she took him in. No doubt she found him just as attractive as everyone else did. Smiling, he handed over the flowers. Her mom blushed. It was embarrassing. Then, he firmly shook her dad's hand, offering to help him with the food preparation. Not knowing what he liked, her mom had picked up chicken, salmon, and tofu to kabob on the grill. Her dad graciously accepted his help, and they both stepped outside. To be honest, she was a little worried about leaving them alone together. Hopefully, her dad wasn't giving him the whole "Hurt my daughter and I kill you" kind of speech.

Beaming, her mom said, "These are beautiful! Handsome and thoughtful. That's a hard combo to find."

"Yeah, he's pretty great, right?"

"So far, so good. Honestly, I was beginning to wonder if you were ever going to date. Don't get me wrong; I'm glad you waited. You should hear some of the stories Sharon tells me about Julie! That girl is a wild one!"

Laughing, she said, "Be grateful I spared you that kind of stress."

Her mom went on. "Just remember, now that you started, it's not a race to the finish. There's nothing wrong with taking things slow. If you ever need to talk about anything, I'm here."

Amused, she rolled her eyes. "Mom, is this a quasi sex talk we're having right now? Because I think we covered the basics two years ago when you pulled out that anatomy book and scarred me for life! Seriously, we're all good!"

Giggling, her mom said, "I guess I was going for shock and awe!"

"Yeah, well, mission accomplished. Did you ever think maybe that's why I didn't date until now?"

They were both hysterically laughing by the time the guys came back in, carrying plates overflowing with food.

"Dinners ready!" her dad called out, "And good news! Kade likes everything!"

They all settled around the dining table, where conversation flowed easily. Kade told them about his family and future college plans. The latter had both of her parents practically eating out of his hand. While they were talking, she took a moment to glance around at her mom, dad, and finally, at Kade. After everything she'd been through, she still wasn't sure exactly what she believed in as far as God was concerned, but for now, she had found faith. Faith in all the people at this table. Faith that her parents loved her. Faith that Kade would always be there for her. Faith that Samuel would always watch over her. Faith in her friends, Kat, Liv, and Gabe, who accepted her and selflessly offered help her when she needed it most.

But, most importantly, faith in herself. It didn't matter if she was confused about God. All that mattered was that she had faith in something. That she believed in something. The past two weeks had opened her eyes to a world far beyond the one she knew. She had witnessed vile and evil things but had also found love. Love was what surrounded her now. She believed in love!

After dinner, Kade said his goodbyes to her parents, and after a lot of gushing, Ava headed up to her room. As she tucked herself in, she noticed the charred book on her nightstand. Smiling, Ava thought about how ironic it was that paranormal romances had always been her favorite reads when her real-life had turned out to be one. The book would serve as a permanent reminder of everything she'd been through. Not that she needed it since she had a real-life person to remind her of it every day. She closed her eyes, picturing Kade's perfect face.

In the dream, she was standing in the middle of a bedroom. As her eyes focused, she realized it was a very messy room that clearly belonged to a boy. The bed was unmade, and the walls were covered in a collage of band posters, pictures, movie stubs, and string lights. The whole motif was a bit overwhelming.

"It worked!" a familiar voice said right behind her.

Startled, she whirled around to find Kade standing there.

Confused, as usual, she asked, "What worked? What's going on?"

Pulling her into his arms, he said, "Looks like I still have some of my powers."

Laying her head against his chest, she asked, "What are you going on about?"

Talk about a good dream. Kade felt so real!

"For old times' sake, I tried to dream-walk. I didn't think it would work, but here you are!"

She still wasn't getting it. "What exactly happened?"

Stepping back, he looked down at her. "Remember when we first met? I told you that when you sleep, I can connect to you and make you see what I see?" she nodded.

"Well, you're asleep right now in your bed. I'm connecting my soul to yours, and you're seeing what I see, like that time in the castle when you woke up in my bed, remember?"

"Oh!" she said, surprised and suddenly a little nervous to be in his room, so close to his bed. A bed he was currently walking her over to. He must have felt her apprehension and stopped.

"Why do you look so scared? Nothing is going to happen that you don't want to happen. Plus, I'd rather our first time be in person and not in a dream."

As they laid down on top of his sheets, he pulled her in close to snuggle, but true to his word; he didn't try anything else. She was thankful for his patience. Right now, she wasn't ready. Just lying in his arms was enough. It was perfect. He was perfect. They talked for hours about nothing and everything. He told her about his childhood, and she did the same. She still didn't know so many things about him, but she was excited to learn it all. Without realizing it, Samuel had given them their own in-between. A private place where no one else could touch them. For the first time since coming back from Purgatory, she felt some of her anxiety over the future melt away. Kade knew the real her. If she sprouted wings or stopped aging, he would help her through it. After several hours passed, she began to feel sleepy, which was ridiculous since her body was technically already asleep. This dream walking stuff was going to take some getting used to. Kissing her goodnight, he finally let go of the connection. Feeling his warmness disappear, she re-opened her eyes to find herself tucked into her bed. Her heart was filled with love as she fell back to sleep, feeling whole and content for the first time in her life.

The End

Epilogue

The following Saturday...

Ava piled into Gabe's SUV with the rest of her friends for the re-do trip to Devils Head Lake. In light of her non-birthday celebration the week before, her friends had gone all out, even decorating the back of the SUV in bold white lettering that read, "Happy Birthday!"

When they pulled up to the lake, Kade gave her a knowing glance, taking her hand in his. It was so weird to be back after all they'd been through. This place had changed both of their lives, for the good and bad. After scarfing down two birthday cupcakes, courtesy of Liv, she and Kade excused themselves to take a walk. Somehow, they ended up walking out on the dock. Standing there, staring out to where the portal sat gave her a sense of unease. She knew Amon was gone, but it was still alarming to know a portal to another world was right there, just under the water's glossy surface.

"It's really beautiful here. Even with, you know!" Kade said, gesturing towards the water.

He was right. The lake was breathtaking with all that turquoise water, reflecting the white-tipped mountains around it. They stood there, hand in hand, taking it all in. Suddenly, Ava felt a weird vibration under her feet. It was there one second and then gone the next. She looked over at Kade, but he didn't seem to notice. Get a grip, she thought. Everything was fine. The lake was just bringing back bad memories. Just as she settled down her thoughts, the vibration happened again. This time, Kade's headshot in her direction. Yup, he definitely felt that one, she thought. Trying to ease both of their minds, she said,

"Look at how old and rickety this dock is. It's probably just straining under our combined weight."

Kade opened his mouth to respond as the water in front of them burst upwards towards the sky. Horrified, they watched as a fountain of shadows exploded from the portal! The shadows spilled out from the frothing water like oil, building up until the blue sky was completely blocked out by a wall of darkness. Growling and whispering, the horde descended upon them. Too rattled to think about the consequences, she grabbed Kade and flashed them both back to the blanket where Liv and Gabe were sitting. She bent down to take Liv's hand, just as Kade grabbed onto Gabe's shoulder. Liv didn't even notice them appear out of thin air. Instead, her big brown eyes were filled with horror as she watched the wall of evil moving in. Oh God, she thought, this was really happening.

Linking them all together, she tried to flash out, but nothing happened. Panicked, she looked at Kade, and he shook his head. Flashing wasn't one of the powers he'd kept, or his ability wasn't working either. They had no time for a plan B. Hearts pounding, they grabbed their friends and ran as fast as they could towards the car.

About the Author

Angela Dunham is the author of the of the Chronicles of the Fallon One Series.

Angela lives in Orlando with her husband and young son and would describe herself as a child chasing, yoga loving, wine enthusiast, who loves to write dark fantasy novels with snarky but lovable characters.

For promotions, release information and freebies, follow her on Social Media

www.authorangeladunham.com

www.facebook.com/AuthorAngelaDunham

www.instagram.com/authorangeladunham/

Facebook Group: Angela's Audience

If you enjoyed The In-Between, pick up these other titles by Angela Dunham:

The Crossing Over

The Hereafter

The Gathering – Short story, The Dark Assent

Copyright

This is a work of fiction. Any references to historical events, real people or real places are fictitious. Other names, characters, places, and events are products of the author's imagination, and any resemblance to actual events or places or persons, living or dead, is entirely coincidental.

Copyright © 2017 by Angela Dunham

Printed in the United States of America

First printing 2018

ISBN 978-0-692-05344-7

All rights reserved, including the right to reproduce this book or portions thereof in any form whatsoever.

For information contact angiedunham@gmail.com

Made in the USA
Columbia, SC
19 March 2022